S C A R S

Steven D. Spratt and Lee G. Spratt

Copyright © 1993 by Steven D. Spratt and Lee G. Spratt

Strawberry Hill Press
3848 S.E. Division Street
Portland, Oregon 97202-1641

No part of this book may be reproduced by any mechanical, photographic, or electronic process, or in the form of a phonographic recording, nor may it be stored in a retrieval system, transmitted, or otherwise copied for public or private use—other than for "fair use"—without the written permission of the publisher.

Cover by Ku, Fu-sheng, based on the cover concept of the authors
Typeset and designed by Wordwrights, Portland, Oregon
Proofread by L. Ann Porter
Vietnam campaign ribbon provided by The Raven Antiques & Military, Portland, Oregon

Manufactured in the United States of America

Library of Congress Cataloging-in-Publication Data

Spratt, Steven D., 1950-
    Scars / Steven D. Spratt and Lee G. Spratt.
      p.   cm.
    ISBN 0-89407-107-6 (paper) : $9.95
      1. Vietnamese Conflict, 1961-1975—Fiction. 2. Vietnamese Conflict, 1961-1975—Veterans—United States—Fiction.
I. Spratt, Lee G., 1959- . II. Title.
PS3569.P673S27   1992
813'.54—dc20   92-19008
                                                                                 CIP

Dear Dad:
I'm writing to you personally because I need some advice only you can give me. I killed a man today. I know I'm in a war and all that, and I've shot at a lot of people while I was here, but this was different.
I wish you were here so you could tell me what to do. I've never said this much, but I love you, Pop, and I have a lot of respect for you. I just hope I manage to get back and see you and Mom again.

The morning newspaper carried the story under two-inch banner headlines: "SOLDIER SLAIN, TWO OTHERS WOUNDED." It told the tale of a young wife, widowed by the war, who'd been determined not to hurt alone.

"Your daddy is gone forever."
"But when will he be coming back?"
"He won't be, not ever."
"But he said he'd come back. He promised."
"I know he promised, honey. I know he said he'd be back. But he's dead, now. He didn't want it this way, but it happened."

"When I get out of here next week, me and my brother are going to start a cattle ranch up in Wyoming. George, that's my brother, he knows everything there is to know about cattle ranching. He even worked on one a couple summers back. That was before he went to jail, though. Is George still in jail?" he asked.
I didn't know what to say. His brother's name had been Philip. Philip was dead, killed in Vietnam ten years earlier.

It was the last sound I registered for a year-and-a-half. When I did wake up, I didn't know my own name. I didn't remember anything of my past. All that came back later.
The doctors said this was progress.

"That was my best friend, lady. I think what you did was a mighty good thing. Thank you, from Thomas."
She requested a change of ward the following morning, and never saw the man who'd spoken to her from the darkness.

ACKNOWLEDGMENTS

No book is written in a vacuum, and without the assistance of the people closest to us, *Scars* would never have seen print. In particular, thanks to the Spratts (especially Ray and Chris) and the Gaylords (especially Alta Mae and Bill); K.W. and Geri Jeter, whose encouragement kept us (reasonably) sane and writing; Jean-Louis and Fu-sheng, whose tea and sympathy saw us through many a dark hour; and, traveling back quite a few years, to Larry Steven Ellis, wherever he may be—thanks, Eli!

DEDICATION

Over sixty thousand Americans either died or were reported missing in action during the years of the Vietnam conflict. Our country owes a tremendous debt to these brave men and women—a debt only partially expiated by the spattering of memorials being erected across the country.

Two-and-a-half-million men and women fought, sweated, and worked through their time in hell...then came home to a nation which reviled them for their efforts. We owe these people a debt also, a debt not yet fully recognized.

Millions more have learned, however slowly and painfully, that the young man or woman they saw go off to war was not the same person after Vietnam.

We dedicate these pages to those who came back—and to the parents, spouses, children and other loved ones who found a stranger in their midst—a stranger who taught them that the worst scars of the war could only be seen with the heart.

PROLOGUE

A Veteran's View

For most of my generation, the Vietnam war is like a bloated, stinking corpse riding the twisting currents of a murky river. Most of the time (if we're lucky), it floats along below the surface, only bumping into the rocks of our subconscious every now and again. But sometimes, when we least expect it, that obscene corpse swirls to the surface and belches forth a foul cloud of gas which threatens to engulf our entire sense of who we are.

In those moments, we feel so alone, so angry, so damn outraged, that we want to lash out at anyone, to blame anyone, to just fight back against the tide of everything wrong about how the war was treated and viewed by what seems like the entire rest of the world.

And when we do lash out, our anger seems to fall on those closest to us. Not our intention, to be sure, but it does anyway.

To those I have lashed out at in my anger and frustration, I apologize—and offer this collection of stories as at least a partial explanation of why my own version of hell (the act of coming home to a society of my peers who reviled me, and learning to fulfill the expectation that I was a pariah) made me into the man I was for over fifteen years. I was angry, confused, and ready to be cast out.

These stories helped me to understand myself, to come to terms with the war, to put it all behind me.

Or so I thought—until today. Today I picked up a Vietnam campaign ribbon for use on the cover of this book, the first time I had held one in my hands for twenty years. To my horror, the war I had so carefully put behind me, the anger I had so carefully laid aside, rose to the surface like that bloated, stinking corpse and once more belched that foul gas over my world.

That's the real world—for me and for millions of others who survived the tragedy of that war. We didn't choose it. We didn't manufacture it.

We just try to live within it.

S.D.S.

To Love a Vet

When the Vietnam war ended, I was fifteen years old. I thought I knew quite a bit about the war—after all, like the rest of the country, I'd been served body counts with dinner for most of my life. I had a brother and a brother-in-law who were both in the service and they knew others who had gone to Vietnam.

Eight years later, I fell in love with a Vietnam vet. He is my second husband, and I am his third (and last!) wife. He is the gentlest man I've ever known, with the greatest capacity for violence. Two years after we met, we stumbled onto our mutual love of writing and decided to give the dream a chance.

The stories you are about to read are fiction. A dozen years after Steve came home to a country that didn't want to acknowledge the Vietnam veteran, our writing began a catharsis which has broken the wall of ice the war placed around his memories and emotions.

Every man, woman and child who loves a Vietnam veteran deals with the changes wrought by that experience in every aspect of their lives together. We hope this book will help open new lines of communication for those marked by the war, and those who deal with its scars every day.

L.G.S.

TABLE OF CONTENTS

Silver Star	13
But...	17
Preserves	21
Bullshit Eddie	29
Setting the Past to Rest	33
Freedom Bird	39
Adam's Dream	43
Mai Lin	47
The Stranger	53
My Brother Says	57
Have You Seen Mary?	59
Conversation in a Bathroom	69
Devil's Dance	73
A Penny for Your Thoughts	77
The Fishing Trip	79
Ticker Tape	83
Western Union	87
You Know I Do	91
The Professor	95
I Hate John Wayne	99
Something to Live With	101
The Goat	105
Heroes	109
Hello, Grant	113
Flame Out	117
Jimi	119
Vigil	125

Silver Star

"I had another dream last night, Doc."
"Why don't we talk about that, then?"
"I don't want to. Not just yet. Maybe later."
"What do you want to talk about?"
"I eavesdropped on some of the guys I work with yesterday. Not on purpose, I was in a stall in the bathroom, and they were both taking a leak. One of them was talking about how tough it was in 'Nam."
"Was it?"
"Yeah. I mean it wasn't anything like what he was saying, but yeah—it was tough."
"What was tough about it?"
Silence.
"He was talking about how he'd humped his ass all over the boonies, nothin' but hard time—but I could tell."
"You could tell what?"
"He was lying. I mean, it wasn't like that at all."
"What was it really like?"
"You know, I bet he's all fucked up in his head."
"Because he lied about Vietnam?"
"Yeah."

"So, what was it like?"

"It was rotten! Stinking, lousy, filthy, crawly, sweaty...rotten. All the time. If we weren't walking, we were fighting somebody we couldn't see so we could walk."

"Isn't that what he was saying?"

"Yeah, but..."

"Yeah, but what?"

"But that's not the way...I mean, he made it sound like it was...I mean, I was there, dammit."

"What was it like when you were there?"

"He got me to thinking about it. Then that damn dream woke me up in the middle of the night. It was so...I mean it was just like I was right back there. I couldn't get it out of my head. So I got up and..."

"And what?"

"I couldn't find my Silver Star."

"You'll have to speak louder. I couldn't hear you."

"I can't find my Silver Star."

"Maybe you misplaced it."

Silence.

"I'm sorry, go on."

"I've never misplaced anything in my life. I looked for my Silver Star last night and it wasn't there. It just...wasn't there."

"What does that tell you?"

"Doc, I killed four people to get that thing. I crawled around the back side of a machine gun bunker and killed four human beings. I can see it all as plainly as I see you right now."

"What does this have to do with the medal?"

"I can feel the guard of my survival knife getting tangled in the last one's clothes, hear it as I rip it free to thrust it into his back again and again. I can still feel the blood, hot on my hands, then cooling as the breeze hits it. I can feel it. I can see it. I can damn near taste it."

"You haven't answered me."

"Yes, I have. You just haven't been listening."

"I can't hear you when you talk that low."

"I said, 'Yes, I have!'"

Silence.

"I'm sorry. I didn't mean to yell at you."

"You still haven't answered me."

"I've found other times where my memory was wrong, at least my memory about Vietnam. I couldn't find my Silver Star because it never happened."

"Are you so certain?"

"Yes. It's not listed in my personnel records at Fort Benjamin Harrison. I called this morning."

"So, your mind painted you a picture to take the place of something else, is that it?"

"I don't know. It's so real."

"But you just told me you'd proven it wasn't real."

"I did. I know it wasn't real. It couldn't have been real. Except..."

"What's the problem?"

Silence.

"Talk to me, Mike."

"I can still feel the blood on my hands."

But...

Sam pulled the door of the phone booth tightly closed behind him, effectively blocking out most of the evening traffic noises. His guitar case took up so much room he could hardly get the door to close. He pulled a crumpled page torn from the public library's copy of the Denver phone book out of his pants pocket and smoothed it on the side of the booth.

There were thirty-seven names highlighted on the paper. Thirty-seven listings for Farmer. Nineteen of these had been marked off with an ink pen. He looked at number twenty and dialed as he pulled handful after handful of change from his pockets.

He started stacking the change in neat piles, each worth a dollar. Twenty nickels, ten dimes, four quarters. The pennies, half-dollars, and the two one-dollar bills he stuffed back into his pockets. They wouldn't fit into the phone.

The line came alive and buzzed in his ear. He poked a finger of his right hand into his ear to further cut off the outside noise. He didn't want to miss a word. The operator's voice came on: "How are you billing this call?"

"I'll pay for it here, Operator."

"That'll be one dollar and forty cents, please." He dropped

the five quarters, one dime and one nickel into the slot. "Thank you." The phone rang and his heart raced.

The phone rang a second time, then a third. Before it could ring the fourth time, it was picked up. "Hello?" It was a woman's voice, white, middle-aged, tired. Sam had a very good ear for voices.

"I-is Dancin' Dan there?"

"Who?"

"Dancin' Dan Farmer. Is he there? This is long distance." He couldn't help it. The fear rose in his throat, making him whine like that. "I gotta talk to him. Is he there?"

"I've never heard of him. There's no Dancin' Dan here."

"But he has to be. I've called so many places. He has to be." The phone went dead in his hand. "Oh, please, don't hang up on me like all the rest."

He checked his list again, then dialed the next name on the list. Another dollar-and-forty cents. The piles were shrinking. On the second ring he got, "Hello. Farmer residence."

"Is Dancin' Dan there, Dancin' Dan Farmer?"

"You must have the wrong number."

"Do you know him? He was my sergeant in 'Nam, and I been looking for him."

"I'm sorry, no. I have never heard of Dancin' Dan. Good night."

"But..." The line was again dead. He drew a line through the name and dialed the next.

Another buck-forty. Seven rings as he crossed his fingers like he'd done so many times before, then a woman's voice. She was young. That's all he could tell for sure. "Hello."

"Is Dancin' Dan there?" The words came out in a rush. He wanted to say it all before she could say that Dancin' Dan wasn't there. "He was my sergeant in..." She cut him off anyway.

"Who is this? Is this some kind of a joke or something? If it is, I think it's really sick." Her voice was shaking with anger.

"No, I'm not joking. He was my sergeant in 'Nam, and I need to talk to him. He always let me talk to him, not like the others."

"Who is this?"

"I'm Sam Simpson. I don't expect he would mention me or nothing, but..."

"Then you really don't know?"

"Don't know what?" The fear made him whine again.

He could hear her swallow, then take a deep, shaky breath. "Dan's dead. He died in Vietnam. He was killed by a mortar blast just before he got on the plane home. That was nearly three years ago."

"No! He couldn't be. He spent two years there. Two years without a scratch. He can't be dead." Sam was openly sobbing now.

"I remember your name. Dan talked about you like you were his best friend." It was not exactly true, but close enough.

"We were buddies. H-h-he took care of me. He helped me with everything. He taught me how to shoot, you know. And he taught me how to walk so the boots didn't blister my feet. A-and he taught me how to hide when the VC were around. He was my friend."

She heard the singular in the word 'friend.' "He wrote me about you, you know?"

"I wrote to my mom about him until she died and he made me stop. He said she couldn't write back any more, but it always made me feel better."

"I'd like to be your friend, Sam." She remembered how Dan had written about stopping the others from calling him Sammy just because he was a little slower than the rest of them.

Sam didn't seem to've heard her. "He can't be dead, he just can't be. I need to talk to him."

"Where are you, Sam?"

"I'm in a phone booth."

"What town are you in?"

The operator said: "Ninety cents for three more minutes, please." She was gone before the woman could say, "Charge it to me at this number, please."

"No! I got money, and I'll pay for it."

"All right, Sam," she soothed. "You can pay for it. Where are you?"

"I'm in Newark, the one in New Jersey." He seemed proud to have remembered.

"Will you come to see me, Sam? I'd really like that. You could tell me about Dan."

"He was supposed to be on the first plane, you know. He was supposed to go first and he made me take his place. He was always doing stuff like that."

"Would you come out and see me, Sam, maybe stay with me for a little while? That way, you could tell me all about Dan and you."

"If he'd taken the first plane, he would still be alive, huh?"

"Don't think about it like that, Sam. Think about the good times you had."

"But he was my friend."

"He really liked you, Sam, he really did."

"But I miss him so much."

"Me, too, Sam. I miss him so much, too. We were only married for a short time, but I loved him so much. Would you please come out to see me, Sam? You could stay with me for awhile and everything."

Sam nodded. "I'll take a bus."

"I can send you money for the ticket if you need it."

"No." He was firm, even sharp. "I'll earn it my ownself. And I'll be there as soon as I can." He hung up without saying goodbye, catching her in the middle of trying to speak.

Sam scraped the change into his palm, flung open the door of the phone booth, and raced across to the brightly-lit sidewalk across the street. Here was a good place to start earning his money.

He set the guitar case on the ground and lifted the old Gibson from the box. He dug into his pocket for the two dollar bills and tossed them and the change into the open case. Then he carefully folded the page from the phone book and placed it in the pick box that supported the neck of the guitar while it was in the case. Also in the case were a dozen other sheets torn from the phone books of a dozen cities, also folded neatly.

Dan had said he lived out west in one of them big cities. It had only taken a couple years to find him. Sam leaned back against the wall, strummed a mellow chord, and began to sing a mournful ballad. The first passerby dropped a dollar bill into the case. Sam smiled his thanks. At this rate, he'd have enough for a bus ticket real soon. He was sure looking forward to seeing Dancin' Dan again.

Preserves

"Mom, have you seen my old tackle box? I thought it was up in the attic, but I can't find it."

She looked up from the biscuit dough, the oversized wooden roller handed down from her grandmother suddenly still. A dusting of flour decorated a spot above her right ear, mixing in with the gray hair she always wore tied back in a bun. "I think it might be out in the garage. Your father cleaned out the attic last year and moved a lot of stuff out there. Didn't make any sense to me, though. Might's well store it in one place as another, as long as I don't have to trip over it."

"Thanks, Mom." I kissed her on the cheek as I went out.

"Don't you go far now, Daniel. We're havin' breakfast here shortly."

"Sure, Mom," I said as the screen door slammed behind me. It was just like it used to be nearly twenty years ago—her still telling me what to do and when to do it, still railing on about Dad and his funny ways—him still shufflin' things around to suit his whims.

Of course, some were things different now.

Dad had retired and now spent most of his time playing pool with his friends downtown, or taking part in an occasional poker party. Not that he was neglecting Mom or anything, but he had his things to do and enjoyed himself.

Mom was active in the Methodist church, involved in a number of their committees. Like Dad, though, her life centered around their time together.

I was married and had three kids and a good job. I was the youngest of three myself.

My oldest brother, Harry, died in the Vietnam war. He was on his second hitch and was killed trying to save another man's life. At least that's what the Army said when they called to tell us of his addition to the body count. I could never understand why one man would throw himself on a grenade in order to save another man's life. I always thought you should take care of yourself first, then others.

Jason thought so, too. He was my middle brother. He'd been to Vietnam, too. I was always sneakily grateful for that. Him being there was enough to keep me from having to see what it was like first-hand. With Harry dead, and Jase over there, I was exempted from having to go to war. Suited me just fine.

I hadn't seen Jason for nearly ten years, now. Used to be, we'd write every once in a while, or talk on the phone, but he'd dropped out of sight and I didn't know him well enough, nor care enough to try to find him. He was a cold and distant man with horrible flashes of fierce temper, and I didn't like him being around the kids. He'd never done anything to hurt one of them or anything, but I just didn't trust him.

I stopped in the middle of the garage and reached up for the rope attached to the ladder. It swung down easily, just like it always had. It was one of Dad's projects from about ten years ago, and led up into the attic of the garage.

I stopped at the top of the ladder and looked around. The room was dark after the bright morning sunshine. It had changed a lot in the last year. Dad'd put an old carpet down over the rough plywood floor. The jumble and clutter that used to overflow from every corner had been picked up, cleaned up, and sorted out into a whole bank of new storage cupboards he must've built.

I flipped the light switch and looked around me. It was amazing, really. He'd lugged a chair up the ladder and set it up in one corner. A reading lamp stood behind it, and an end table scarred by coffee-cup rings sat to the right. It seemed to be a retreat of some sort.

I looked around a minute more, then set about searching for that tackle box. I'd promised the kids I'd take them fishing after breakfast, so I had to find that box. Marti and I brought our kids out to my parents' farm each year for my birthday, and each year I made the same promise.

The first two cupboards really surprised me. I'd expected to find things from the dusty past and instead I found row upon row of Mason jars filled with all sorts of brightly-colored preserved fruits and vegetables, glistening clean and neatly ordered. There must have been more than two hundred of them stacked on shelves from the floor to the ceiling.

I closed the two doors and opened the next pair. They were just as neat and clean, and were filled with more of the type things I'd expected to find here. I pawed through them, looking for the tackle box, and almost immediately came across my old baseball glove. It was well-oiled, the leather still soft after all this time.

A nick in the little finger made me think about the time I saved the game with a diving catch at the fence. It was just a sandlot game, but I'd been proud. So proud that I hadn't made a sound as Mom painted iodine on all the scratches I'd gotten from the barbed wire.

I set the glove back on the shelf and checked the next cupboards. More of the same, and all of it strangely neat and orderly. My home had always been clean, but lived in, while I was growing up. This was almost like a museum.

On the bottom right shelf, under a shoe box, I found the tackle box. It, too, had been cleaned up from what I remembered. It shone like new. I opened it to see if all my flies and lures were still there. They were, but I'd never left them all orderly like that.

Suddenly the shoe box slipped from the shelf I'd set it on and dropped. The lid popped off on impact and the contents spilled out on the floor. It was filled with letters, old letters.

I dimly remembered seeing the box a couple years before. Mom had given it to Dad and asked him to put it in the attic with "all the rest of the junk you keep hanging around here." She'd called him a packrat, pushed it into his hands and nudged him along on his way.

I started gathering the letters together so I could put them back in the box. Then something struck me as odd. There were postmarks, but no stamps. Instead, the word "Free" was written in the upper right corner of each of the envelopes. It took a minute for that to sink in, for me to realize that they had been mailed from Vietnam.

I picked the box of letters up and carried them over to the chair. When I'd got myself seated, I started to put them in order by the postmarked dates. It only took a couple minutes, since they were mostly in order anyway.

I didn't know the handwriting, so I figured they had to've come from Harry. I'd written back and forth with Jase enough times to know this wasn't his angular script.

I picked up the first one. It was postmarked in July of 1966. I thought for a minute and figured out that Harry would have just turned eighteen at the time. That meant Jase was almost fifteen, and I was twelve.

"Dear Mom and Family," it began in an almost childish scrawl. "I'm at Oakland Army Base. I've just got a couple minutes before another formation. They have one every two hours around the clock. You just keep going to the formations until your name is called, then you pack up and leave. I wish they'd hurry up and get it over with. I'm scared enough without this kind of torture."

I tried to bring up a picture of Harry in my mind, but found it wouldn't come. It had been too long since I had seen my brother. All I got was a vague image of him being much taller than I was and having a deep voice.

The letter continued in a different colored ink. "I'm back. They called my name this time. In two hours, I'll be on a flight to Vietnam. I don't know yet, but I think we'll be stopping in Alaska on the way. Write more later. Love to you all, and tell Miney to wipe his nose."

I'd forgotten all about that. Mom had introduced us as Eeney, Meeney, and Miney one time. When she was asked where Moe was, she looked over the top of her glasses and said, "There ain't goin' to be no Moe!" The names stuck, and I was often called Miney after that. Jase was Meeney, but I thought at the time it was because of his temper.

"Dear Mom and Family." The next letter was just as short, and postmarked a week later. "We landed at Cam Rhan Bay yesterday and I've been going steady ever since. I used to think it was hot back home, but it is really hot here. When we landed, it was 106 degrees and the humidity was 99%. That's hot in anybody's book. Gotta run now. I'll let you know as soon as I get a permanent address. Love you all."

I read through several more letters, all short, all warm. Then I came across one addressed to Dad at his old work address. The postmark said it had been mailed in January of '67. The handwriting on this one was different. It was compact, precise, as if it were carefully drawn letter by letter. It was longer than any of the others.

"Dear Dad." The salutation was blurred and you could still see the erasure marks where Harry had been trying to make up his mind about how to start the letter.

"I'm writing to you personally, because I need some advice only you can give to me. I killed a man today. I know I'm in a war and all that, and I've shot at a lot of people while I was here, but this was different.

"He was no more than ten feet away, and looking right at me when I pulled the trigger. His face showed surprise and pain, but no fear at all. Every time I close my eyes, I see him looking at me, smiling a small smile. Blood is running out of all the holes I put in his chest. I can't go to sleep or anything. I don't know what to do. I don't know how to cope with it.

"I wish you were here so you could tell me what to do. I've never said this much, but I love you, Pop, and I have a lot of respect for you. I just hope I manage to get back and see you and Mom again."

Just then, I heard Dad clear his throat, and I looked up. He'd somehow managed to make it to the top of the ladder without me hearing him, and was standing there looking embarrassed with his hands in his pockets.

He took off his glasses and swiped at the tears standing in the corners of his eyes with a dirty handkerchief. He had to clear his throat twice more before he could speak, then his voice was still tight with controlled emotion.

"Your mother says breakfast is ready." I folded the letter and put it back in the envelope. Dad settled himself down to the floor and took a couple deep breaths before he started talking again.

"I've raised three sons. They're the crop of my life." He was talking real slow and quiet. I had to strain to follow him. "They're all three good boys, each in their own way."

It was like he was explaining things to a stranger.

"My first boy, Harold, went away to war and became an old man before he was twenty." He gestured at the letter in my hand. "He found out what it meant to kill another human being. Not to murder in anger but to kill a stranger just because he was told to. It made him far older than his years. He learned to see the larger picture. He learned the futility of war first-hand, and went one step further."

He stopped and wiped at his eyes again. I watched him, but he never met my gaze.

"He learned that he could make a difference by saving lives, that he could put a dent into the stupidity of war. That lesson cost him his life in the '68 Tet Offensive, and cost me my first-born son."

His voice steadied into an iron monotone. "It also cost me my second son. He was so furious at the death of the older brother he idolized that he volunteered to go over there just so he could even the score. We found out that he'd joined the Army even before Harry's funeral.

"He paid a big price, too. He lost most of his humanity, his acceptance of people's weaknesses. He can't accept himself or the people around him."

Dad raised his head and looked at me. The pain in his eyes was a deep pit, an open wound that had festered for nearly two decades. He went on in the same metallic monotone. "My third son has made his mark on the land. He has a family of his own, and a place in the world."

His face twisted and tears ran down his cheeks as he continued. "Your mother and I come up here often. Sometimes her, sometimes me. We've never been able to face it together, her and me. We feel the loss, but we don't know how to talk about it." He took another swipe at his eyes.

I wanted to say something, something that would make everything all better, but I was helpless. I had no idea of what to say. I opened my mouth, then closed it again.

His eyes bored into me. "I never said it to any of you boys, God knows why not, but I love you, son. I love you more than I'll ever have the words to say it with."

He lunged to his feet and stumbled down the steps of the ladder. I didn't realize it until he was gone, but I was crying just as hard as he'd been.

I sat there a few minutes longer, holding Harry's letter in my hand. Then Mom's voice was raised in the house. "Daniel, you come down here this instant! Your breakfast is getting cold."

I dropped the letter back into the box with the others and set it gently on the shelf where it'd been. I picked up the tackle box and took one last look around before I turned off the light and made my way back out into the morning sunshine.

Bullshit Eddie

Bullshit Eddie was known in every bar within seventeen blocks of his room at the Excelsior Hotel. Some said he had been living there when it was built, camped in a dumpster full of packing material, and they figured it would be easier to just put the building up around him. When Bullshit Eddie heard the story, he just grinned what he figured was a sly grin and winked his good eye.

The left leg of his jeans hung empty below the knee, but that didn't slow him down much. He could make better time on his crutches than most men could do running with two good legs. Some people felt sorry for him, tried to do for him, but not me. I figured him for a dirty-necked loser who'd rather cadge a drink than try to get ahead.

I was sitting in Molotov's, working on getting on the outside of my third bourbon and coke. It was a quiet Saturday afternoon, and I was enjoying being alone in the middle of a bunch of people. Every once in a while I'd get a friendly nod, or a hello from somebody I knew, but I could still enjoy my own space.

A commotion started at the front door and worked its way down the length of the bar. I grabbed a handful of wheels and swung around to see what was happening. Sure enough, it was

Bullshit Eddie glad-handing his way along. He slapped backs, shook hands, and grinned through his broken teeth like he was running for office. I spun the chair back to my table in disgust. If there's anything in this world I can't stand, it'd have to be either a politician or a panhandler. Bullshit Eddie was both.

Eddie had his third drink in his hand without ever touching his pocket by the time he pulled to a stop at my table. "How you doin' today, my man?"

"Bullshit Eddie." I let my feelings show in the simple statement. His eyes narrowed a bit, but he should be used to it by now. He knew I didn't like him, or his way of getting by. I'd lost the use of both my legs when a VC sniper's bullet had shattered my spine just above the hips, but I had a career and my self-respect. If you listened to Eddie, you never knew—really knew—for sure how he managed to lose the eye and the half-a-leg. One time it was a logging accident, another it was a motorcycle wreck. I doubt if he really knew for sure.

"You got no call to talk to me in that tone of voice, Stanley. I ain't done nothin' to you." I think I hated that whining of his more than anything else. Even it was bullshit. His voice changed, went more nasal, but the expression in his one eye never wavered a bit.

I glared at him. "Why don't you just get the hell away from me and leave me the..."

"Nobody move! This is a stickup!"

A young man, stringy blond hair, skinny as a skeleton was standing just inside the front door. He held a shiny pistol in his left hand, waving it at us. I'd never seen him before. I did what I was told, not that I could have been a danger to him in my wheelchair. Everybody else did the same.

Everybody, that is, but Eddie. He turned slowly on his one whole leg and faced the newcomer. A big grin of welcome split his stubbled face. "Freddie! Good to see you again, my man." He began to stump his way over toward the hold-up man, talking steady.

"My name's not Freddie, and I ain't no friend of yours, so back off, crip, before I blow off your other leg." The kid was shifting around nervously, rubbing the pit of his left elbow with the heel of his right hand.

"Need a pop pretty bad, don't you, Freddie? You'd have to need it pretty bad to try something like this." Eddie was talking soft and low and moving slowly ahead, hitching along the floor with his crutches. He was no more than ten feet away when he went on. "I've got some, you know. I got the spike and everything. I don't mind sharing."

The kid started to swing the pistol around to cover Bullshit Eddie. Eddie took another slow hitch along the floor and was less than eight feet away. I noticed I was sweating as much as the junkie.

"Let's go back into the bathroom and get us a pop, how about it?" That wheedling nasal tone sounded different, somehow.

"I told you to get the hell away from me!" the kid shouted and swung the pistol the rest of the way toward Eddie. The sound of the shot was deafening in the room. Eddie lunged in as the bullet took him in the chest. He swung the tip of his right crutch up, dropped the left one, and nailed the kid just below the jaw with a straight, spear-like jab. They both hit the floor at the same time. Neither was moving.

Somebody from down the bar kicked the pistol away from the kid's hand and knelt down to check his pulse. He looked up, face pale, and said, "He's dead. Eddie killed him with his goddamn crutch."

They were rolling Eddie over by the time I could get my chair over there. They peeled back his shirt to get a look at the wound. It always seems like such a small hole, too small to kill a man, but he was as dead as he would ever be.

His shirt fell open further as I got close enough to see. Bullshit Eddie had been shot before. A neat row of three small puckered scars stretched from his belt to just below his collarbone. From the spacing, I could see that the fourth was probably the one that took out his eye.

A grimy leather shoelace encircled his neck, holding a ribbon with a piece of metal attached. I reached down and turned it over. It was a Distinguished Service Cross.

Setting the Past to Rest

The phone rang once, twice—then a third time. Greg shifted his weight from foot to foot, nervously lighting another cigarette even though one burned in his ashtray.

It rang a fourth time, an impatient buzz in his ear. His heart nearly stopped when the receiver was lifted. "Hello?"

"Mrs. Hartford?"

"Who's calling?" Her tone was guarded, tense.

"I'm not a salesman, Mrs. Hartford. It's me, Greg."

The next moment stretched to a gossamer fineness. "Greg who?"

He held his temper. After all, he'd been gone for nearly eleven years. He expected resentment. "Greg Fuller."

"Of all the incredible gall!" She slammed the phone down in its cradle.

Greg desperately wanted to call her back immediately, but he knew she would only hang up again. He rose from his chair and went into the kitchen. He pulled a two-liter bottle of sparkling soda from the fridge, his gaze lingering longingly on the lone can of beer at the front of the shelf.

With a practiced resolution, he closed the door and poured the last of the soda into a fresh glass. He recapped the bottle and dropped it into a box at the end of the counter.

That can of beer had been in the same place for two years, nine months, and seventeen days. Each day it tested him, and every day so far he'd won. Not one day had been easy.

He kept a careful eye on the clock. He knew that it would be at least twenty minutes before Mrs Hartford would relax enough to give him a chance to talk. Sometimes it took longer.

He gave it exactly twenty minutes.

The phone was answered on the second ring, hesitantly. "Hello?"

"Please don't hang up, this is very important." The words tumbled out in a rush, each anxious to reach her ears in time to stop the action of her hand. He held his breath. Five seconds. Ten. Fifteen.

"What do you feel is so important that you would have the nerve to call me?"

"I have to talk to Cindy."

"We've covered all this. It's been dead business for ten years. Cindy doesn't want to talk to you."

"Mrs. Hartford, I'm dry. I haven't had a drink in almost three years."

"That's an old song, too, Greg."

"I made a lot of mistakes. I'm trying to set some of them straight."

"She's married, you know."

That shook him. He'd considered it, even expected it, but it hadn't been real.

"You won't cause her trouble, will you?" she asked his silence. "She's had more of that than anybody ever needs."

"That's all I want to tell her."

"I'll tell her for you." By the tone of her voice, she didn't expect that to fly.

"Mrs. Hartford, I am trying to go back and rectify my mistakes. I have to tell her myself."

"There's no way you can fix what you did to her!" She was angry all over again.

He rushed into his reply, trying to keep her from hanging up on him again. "Please! Don't hang up. I know I can't fix it. I might be able to explain it, though. If I can talk to her, that is. Please, Mrs. Hartford."

"I'll give her your number. I'll do that and tell her you called."

"You know she won't call me. I can't say I blame her, either."

"You were a real bastard to her, Greg, a real genuine bastard. You're right. She wouldn't call you, and I wouldn't blame her."

"I wouldn't either. Please help me, Mrs. Hartford. I want to help both of us set the whole thing behind us."

"Call back in an hour. No promises, but I'll try to have her here."

"Thank you. You won't be sorry, I promise."

"We've all had more than enough of your promises, Greg."

That hour was one of the longest Greg had ever spent. He remembered their times together, times of love and laughter, times of violent brawling. He was so nervous the sweat was rolling down his ribs. He finished the glass of soda and went to the fridge for more.

He'd drunk the last of it while on the phone to Mrs. Hartford. Nothing cold remained. Nothing but the lone can of beer staring balefully up at him. He reached a shaky hand out and stroked a finger down its sweaty side. His tongue ached for the cold thrill of it.

He won the battle yet again when he firmly closed the door on his yearnings.

The clock on the wall hummed on, loud in his anxiety. He turned the television on and turned it right back off. The sound jarred him and made him even more restless. He paced the floor, five steps to the hall door and five steps back. He made each turn by the phone stand.

He waited the full hour, waited with shaky hands, then he called.

She picked up the phone halfway through the first ring. "Greg?"

"Yes."

"Fuck you!" She slammed the phone down so hard it hurt his ear.

He dialed again immediately, somehow sensing he was right this time.

She didn't say a word, just listened for a long moment.

"I was wrong."

"Fuckin'-A right you were wrong. You fuckin' walked out on me."

"I know. I can remember it now."

"What's this 'I can remember now,' shit? Are you going to try to tell me you had goddamn amnesia or something?"

"No. I'm not going to tell you that. I'm going to tell you the truth."

"You don't know what the fuckin' truth is, you asshole."

"That's almost right. I *didn't* know what it was. *Didn't*. I'm learning now, a little bit at a time, but learning."

"Right. I believe you. What's this shit about you not drinking?"

"Two years, nine months, and seventeen days. I'm dry."

"For good?"

"I hope so. I just take it one day at a time."

He could feel her relenting the tiniest fraction. "I really am trying to put myself back together, Cindy."

"Bully for you. What do you want me to do, loan you money?"

"No. I want you to try to understand, that's all. I'm not trying to get back into your life, I'm trying to make our past rest easier on both of us."

"If you want to be forgiven, go to confession. That's their gig."

"I'm not asking for forgiveness, Cindy."

"Don't call me Cindy. That's what my friends call me."

"I haven't been in a fight in two-and-a-half years, Cynthia, not even an argument."

"Right."

"It's true."

"You know, I'm married now. I'm not the least bit interested in getting back together with you."

"I know."

"You know a whole hell of a lot, don't you?"

"No, but I'm finally learning."

"Hip-hip-hooray!"

"I treated you badly."

"No shit, Sherlock. You treated me like dirt and then you just fuckin' disappeared. You take off one morning to look for a job and you never come back."

"Would you believe me if I told you I'm sorry?"

"No."

"I am."

"Big fuckin' deal."

"I spent five years in and out of Vet centers. I had to work pretty hard to find out who I am."

"Did you?"

"I'm getting there."

"Good! Now we can both hate you!"

"How can I get around your anger?"

"You can damn well wait eleven years like I did!"

"I want to see you."

"People in hell want ice water, too."

"I really do."

"Not a chance in hell."

"Cindy..."

"Cynthia, asshole. Your name isn't on the list of my friends."

"Cynthia, it took me ten years to leave Vietnam behind."

"That's nice. It only took you ten seconds to leave me behind."

"I didn't know who I was, then. I was just a kid, for Christ's sake, just a kid who grew up in Vietnam. I had no idea what the hell the world was like."

"If you're going to swear at me, I'll just hang up."

"No! Please. Don't hang up. Let me finish."

"You already finished things."

"You're right, I did. I can't fix anything, but I'd like to have you understand."

"I don't care enough to understand."

"I do. I do care. I screwed up everything I touched. I just wanted to tell you that I understand now. I understand how right you were about what I put you through. I understand and I want to tell you I was wrong and I am very sorry for screwing up your life."

"Why are you doing this?"

"I'm calling everybody I screwed up. I know I can't make it right, but I can tell you I know I was very wrong."

"Guinness'll buy that and put it in the section marked 'understatements.'"

"I can't ask you to forgive me, that's too much. Please, just understand that I'm trying to get myself straight."

The clock on the wall hummed loudly while he waited for her to say something. Finally, she spoke. "You're on the level, aren't you? You aren't just stroking me?"

"Yes."

"I guess I wish you well, then. I wish you well, but I can't say I understand why you did all those things you did."

"I don't either, not yet anyhow."

"Can you settle for that?"

"From you, yes, but not from myself."

"Good. That's a start. Keep it up."

"Thanks for listening. It took me a long time to work up my nerve to call you."

"Greg, I understand why you called. Please don't do it again. I don't want to talk to you again. You're a long-forgotten part of the past. Stay there."

"I can do that, now. Goodbye, Cynthia."

"Goodbye, Greg."

He set the receiver gently in the cradle, took a deep breath, and crossed her name off the list. It was not a long list, and hers was the last name to be crossed off. He took a deep breath, shook his head ruefully, and turned off the light.

Now the past could rest.

Freedom Bird

Joel sighed and looked out the window of the DC-10. They were still above the clouds. He couldn't see the easternmost shore of the Pacific Ocean slipping under the fuselage, but he knew it was there. Home at last! Back to the real world! God, what a sound that had.

He turned pensive again. Home? Home had been a plywood hooch, or a sandbagged bunker, or a stomped-down patch of buffalo grass for more than two-and-a-half years now. How was he going to cope with the *real world*? The rules were different.

Joel had been seventeen-years-old when his father signed the papers giving him permission to join the Army. He still remembered the look of pride and the glisten of tears in his father's eyes when he came out of the room where he had been sworn in. They didn't say a word, just shook hands—a long and firm handshake, man to man. Then Joel turned and walked from the room, proud and straight. That was the last time he saw his father alive. He was killed in a car wreck while Joel was still away at basic training.

By the time Joel had returned from his emergency leave, he had decided to build himself into the kind of man his father could always be proud of. He would be the best damn soldier this world had ever known.

Joel came through at the top of his class in Officer Candidate School, then volunteered for the Special Forces and Airborne Training. He did as well there, then volunteered for combat duty in Vietnam. It was a time when the war was gobbling up second lieutenants faster than the Army could turn them out. The word was you'd either die or be promoted within your first month...or both.

Joel looked forward to it, believing his father had been right. It was a man's duty to fight for his country, even die for it if necessary. Over there, he could make his father's memory proud.

Now, two-and-a-half years, seven Purple Hearts, an Army Commendation Medal, two Silver Stars, a Bronze Star, and a Distinguished Service Cross later, he was leaving the war behind him. He was going home.

He could hardly remember what it was like to live in a civilized place. He lay back in his seat and thought of the many things he had missed. Girls, that was first. Girls with round eyes and cream-colored skin. And the smell of a pine tree, he missed that, too. Cars with tops and doors on them. Flush toilets. Paved roads you could walk down without a rifle slung on your shoulder. Drinking water that came from the faucet clear and cold.

His thoughts were interrupted as the pilot's voice came through the speakers, calm and warm. "Gentlemen, we have just crossed the coast of the United States of America. Let me be the first to say—Welcome Home!"

A thunderous cheer rang throughout the plane. Men stamped their feet, screamed their throats hoarse, shook the hands they could reach, and kissed the stews.

Joel just smiled. At two months short of twenty-two, he was one of the youngest captains in the Army. The route he had chosen had destroyed much of his ability to be touched by circumstance. Even coming home was a surface emotion.

The "No Smoking" light and the seatbelt announcement were simultaneous. He stubbed out his cigarette and raised the back of his seat to an upright position. As he buckled the belt, a hush fell throughout the aircraft. The stews moved quietly up the aisle checking each belt with a practiced eye and a professional smile.

Throughout the plane, necks were craned for the first glimpse of the *real world* below. Conversation was tight and subdued, waiting for that first flash of land.

The freedom bird eased down through layer after layer of piled cotton clouds, finally breaking free at about five thousand feet. Below, green and lovely, lay the promised land. The good ol' U S of A.

In the rear of the aircraft, a lone voice started a chant, "We made it! We made it!" It was picked up by nearly every throat in the aircraft. Joel was surprised to find a tear trickling down his cheek. He couldn't remember the last time he had cried over anything.

Louder and louder the chant became. A hundred voices, then nearly two hundred. Men and women hungering for a land without war invoked the spell of freedom with that incantation. They had been born and raised in the USA, but for the most part they had grown up on the LZs and rice paddies of South Vietnam. To his own astonishment, Joel found himself involved in the chant, bellowing and shaking his fists in the air. His carefully-nurtured professional reserve vanished like a puff of smoke.

With each round of the chant, he came closer to realizing that he was really coming home, not leaving it behind. All around him, tears flowed from the eyes of soldiers who had forgotten how to cry. Home was the most beautiful word in the English language.

He looked again—saw the houses slipping by silently under the silver wings of the freedom bird. Cars rolled freely on the streets and freeways. It was the *real world*—that fabled dream land he hardly remembered.

The tires squawked their protest as the plane settled down on the runway, and the engines whined as the thrust was reversed. His hand went to his tie, checking its straightness. He felt scared; good, but scared. It was all going to be so strange.

The plane taxied up to the terminal. He could see the passenger off-loading ramp being pushed out to meet them. No more than a couple of minutes, and he would have his feet on free soil. Home at last!

The plane came to a complete stop, and the captain's voice informed them that a bus would be waiting for them at the other side of the terminal. It would take them to the processing center, where they would receive their paperwork.

The doors were propped open, and Joel was the first to leave the plane. His nostrils flared as the heady scent of wind off the mountains and city exhaust fumes mingled to make a perfume better than any he had ever smelled before. A cluster of people, maybe a hundred in all, were waiting at the foot of the ramp. Families and friends of the passengers, no doubt. He paid them no mind. He'd have nobody here to meet him. This was only the first leg of his journey.

Joel was four steps from the bottom when a young woman, tears streaming down her face, stepped free of the crowd. She raised both hands in front of her, clasping an automatic pistol with white-knuckle tension. Joel saw the pistol, saw it spout flame, but he never felt the bullet hit him in the center of the chest.

The morning newspaper carried the story under two-inch banner headlines: "SOLDIER SLAIN, TWO OTHERS WOUNDED." It told the tale of a young wife, widowed by the war, who'd been determined not to hurt alone.

Adam's Dream

Jenny was seven. She was in second grade. She could do her "timeses" all the way up to the sixes, write her name in cursive, and read better than anybody else in the class. Her long, blond hair fell to nearly her waist in a flaxen waterfall. Her blue eyes sparkled with curiosity about the entire world around her.

Harry was three. He could spell his name and recite his address and telephone number without error. He was that rare individual that could be bathed, dressed in clean clothes, placed alone on a couch, and told not to move. He would obey and be filthy within minutes. Adam had nicknamed him "Dirty Harry" while he was only six months old. The name stuck because it fit so well. Harry was proud of having a two-word name because nobody else had one.

Nancy was twenty-six. She'd married Adam when they were both eighteen and fresh out of high school. He was the only man she'd ever loved and she was the only woman he'd ever been with. They'd both known since sixth grade that they would spend the rest of their lives together.

They'd both known that until today's mail had come. There were two pieces of mail today. One the Army had sent to her, and one she had mailed to Adam in Vietnam. She hadn't opened the first for a while, because the second said it all.

In red ink, stamped across the front of the envelope were the words, "DECEASED—RETURN TO SENDER." The red ink had first caught her attention, then yanked her insides out. She hadn't cried yet. She knew that would come later, but not yet. It just had to be a mistake. Adam was so alive. They had plans. She looked around the tiny apartment and saw the house they had wanted to build together, the home that was to be.

Finally, she opened the letter from the Army. Adam had been killed in action, died a "hero's death." She could "take comfort that he'd served his country well," and, "have pride in him." All she could feel was empty and alone. So empty and alone.

Then Harry woke up from his nap and she had to keep him entertained while she tried to figure out how to tell the children. Jenny arrived from school, bustling with news of her "magnicifent day."

Nancy listened closely, smiling at all the right places, feeling the lack of the joy that had always been there when Jenny told of her exploits.

Supper bought her some more time, but time didn't bring answers. It just made the emptiness echo even more. She rose from the table, leaving most of her dinner untouched, and went into the living room. She called her mother, and when she answered, said, "Please come over now."

"I'll be there in half-an-hour, dear. Is something wrong?"

"Yes. Please come over."

"I'm leaving right now."

She stacked the dishes mechanically, intending to do them later, then gathered Harry and Jenny onto the couch in the living room. They were uncharacteristically subdued, sensing that something was wrong.

When she had one of them safely tucked under each arm, she took a deep breath and began.

"Jenny," she looked at their daughter, their little piece of sunshine. "Harry," she looked at their son, the very promise of deviltry. "I have something very important to tell you." She was astounded by the lack of emotion in her voice.

"Your daddy is gone forever."

"No, he's not, Mommy." This was Jenny. "He's just gone off to fight a war. He'll be coming back."

Adam's Dream

"No, he won't, honey," she stroked her daughter's hair back from her forehead. "He is dead. He was killed in the war."

"But when will he be coming back?"

"He won't be, not ever."

Dirty Harry was silent, a serious expression on his face.

Jenny said, "But he said he'd come back. He promised."

"I know he promised, honey. I know he said he'd be back. But he's dead, now. He didn't want it this way, but it happened."

"You said we should never break a promise."

Harry spoke for the first time. "If I stay real clean, will my daddy come back?"

All Jenny could offer was a hug.

Mai Lin

"John, you come here and look at this. I mean, just you look at this." Mabel was peering out her bedroom window into the back yard. Her husband of nearly forty years came to the window and looked at his son and new daughter-in-law in the back yard.

"Look at what, Mabel?"

"Look at them, you silly old fool. Look how they're crouched down on their heels like some kind of animals instead of sitting over there in a lawn chair."

It was true, they were sitting on their heels instead of a chair. Chris had been doing that a lot ever since he'd come back from Vietnam. He'd been doing it even more since he announced that he and Mai Lin were married. They'd crouch like that and talk for hours in an eclectic mixture of English, Vietnamese, and French, using whatever word suited the situation best. It was hard to follow a conversation between them.

"They look perfectly comfortable to me, Mabel. Come away from the window and let the children have some privacy."

"Privacy," she snorted through her nose, "if they want privacy, let them find their own place and move out. I don't like having that little slanty-eyed woman always hanging on my son like some kind of bitch in heat. I don't like them living here at all. What will the neighbors think, seeing them out in the yard like that?"

"Mabel, just you back off your high horse. What the neighbors think is their own damn business. I look out that window and I see two people in love. I see my son out there, looking more at home and relaxed than I've seen him since he came back from the war. I see him married to a beautiful young woman who thinks the world of him. He thought he'd lost her during the evacuation, but they got back together after almost five years apart. I see a very lucky couple."

"John, we've lived here for thirty years. Thirty years in the same house, with the same neighbors. If you don't care what they think, I sure do. They're my friends."

"And Chris is your son. You tell me which is more important to you." His voice was shaking with outrage, confused by his wife's reactions.

"Don't you try to make me a villain, because I'm not. You know how those people are. She just wants to get his money. Probably smokes that opium, too. They're all alike, every damn one of 'em."

"Mabel, you just put that kind of prejudice out of your mind. I won't have it in my house, not now and not ever. Do you understand me?" He raised his voice to her for only the third time in their thirty-nine years of marriage. "First off, he has no money, not even a job. What money comes in, she brings in from her job."

John took Mabel by the arm and turned her back to the window. "Drugs cost money, too. She uses everything she gets to help out here. Just you look at her. Look at her face, the way she lights up when she looks at our son. Look at the way she reaches out to touch him. Look at his eyes, the love there. Look at it, Mabel. Look at it and then tell me that she's using him."

Mabel shrugged his hand from her arm. "I don't care. She's one of them, not one of us. I look at her, and I see yellow, not white." Her tone was cold and barren.

John drew himself up to his full height and said in a voice just as cold: "In all the time we've been married, I never knew you to hold to a prejudice or to say a mean word against another human being. I don't think I like it. In fact, I don't like it all. I like you a lot less now for you being this way. I'm going to have to think about this. This might just change the whole way I think about you...and us." He turned away from her and went down the stairs and into his basement workshop.

She heard the lock being turned on the door. The snick of the bolt sliding home had a final ring to it, since he'd never locked the door behind him before. In a daze, she went over to her bed and sat on the edge. She couldn't understand why he was acting this way. Everybody knew they were different from normal folks.

Why, they ate food that'd turn your stomach just to smell it. And they dressed different than other people, too. They didn't even try to fit in with good folks, the people who'd made this country so great.

They weren't even Christians, for God's sake. Mai Lin never went to church with her, she always had something else to do. Always found an excuse so she didn't have to become like the rest of us. A heathen, that's what she was, a cursed heathen.

Mabel snatched a tissue from a box at the head of the bed, and blew her nose loudly. She could hear John's gentle voice chiding her, "Must be foggy out today, dear. That ship sounded like it was real close." He always made fun of the loud noise she made when she blew her nose.

She wondered how he could have gotten mad at her over this little thing. Why couldn't he see it when it was as plain as the nose on your face. Him and his damned Irish temper. Always gettin' mad at one thing or another. But that wasn't really true. He was a quiet man, not given to outbursts.

He got upset at a lot of things. He even tried to do something about them sometimes. But he never lost his temper like she did. She'd blow up at the slightest thing, sometimes, but he weathered the storms one after another without ever getting mad at her. *With* her, sometimes, but not *at* her.

"Mom. Mom, are you in here?" It was Chris' voice downstairs.

She wiped her eyes and blew her nose before she answered, "I'm upstairs, Chris."

"Can you come down here? I need to talk to you for a minute." She was straightening her dress as she started down the stairs. Chris was waiting in the living room for her.

"Mom, I've got some news for you." His tone was serious enough that it chased a chill of fear up her spine.

"Is something wrong? Is your father...?"

"No, Mom. Nothing's wrong. At least not like that. Mai Lin and I are moving out. I've got a job that starts Monday, a good job with a future, and we both know how you feel about Mai Lin."

She opened her mouth to object, but he pressed his forefinger across her lips before she could speak. "It's not your fault, Mom. At least it's not your fault you started out feeling this way. We understand, we really do. I just hope you don't feel that way about your grandson."

Mabel pursed her lips until they looked like somebody had pulled a drawstring. "All that talk about a grandson is neither here nor there. A child can't be responsible for the mistakes of his parents. And it's not that I really dislike her, it's just that...did you say 'grandson?'"

Chris grinned from ear to ear. "Yeah. We're gonna have a baby. Mai Lin just found out today that she's pregnant."

"You go out there and tell that girl to come into the house. I want to talk to her."

"Mom, I'm not going to let you make it any worse on Mai Lin than it already is."

"Young man, you just do what your mother told you. Go on, get." She spun him around and punctuated her "get" with a slap on the rear, just like she'd always done when he was little. He got.

A of couple minutes later, they came back through the door. Mai Lin was holding her head high, ready to battle for the man she loved. Mabel was waiting in the middle of the room. She said, "Mai Lin, I've been wrong and treated you horribly. I want to apologize. I was wrong in my attitudes. I can't say I'll change right away, but I'll try real hard. Would you please forgive me?" She opened her arms to receive the girl. They were both crying as they embraced.

Over Mai Lin's shoulder, she said: "You go on downstairs and pry your father out of his workshop. You tell the old fool that we have to start adding a room onto the back of the house so my son and his wife have a place to live until they get on their feet. Go on, scoot."

She turned her attention back to Mai Lin. "How far along are you? We've got a lot of plans to make, you know?" She settled to a sitting position on the floor, drawing the girl after her.

The Stranger

"I still have the clock radio. Of course, it doesn't work anymore. It has a size ten hole where I kicked it. The clock is forever frozen at 5:01 p.m. That's when I heard them announce that Da Nang had been evacuated and turned over to the advancing VC and NVA.

"What I don't have is the next three days. They are gone forever, carried away by the booze I drank trying in vain to fill the hollow sense of outrage and betrayal I felt...still feel."

He paused and drew a shaky breath, rubbing the sweaty palms of his hands on the sides of his faded blue jeans. His eyes were focused on a place we could all see: The years past, the years after the war. We waited while he gathered our feelings for another try at putting them into words.

He continued: "I lost something, then. I lost it and I don't even know what it is. I just know it's gone and I miss it so much it wakes me up in the middle of the night, steals minutes out of my day like some street dip lifting a wallet. It's gone before you know it."

He fought the tears, lost, and scrubbed his eyes with a shirtsleeve. "I find myself crying in the middle of something that isn't reaching me and not knowing why."

He looked up, eyes sparkling in the neon light. He stared at each of us as if he'd never seen us before. It was almost true. We were a veterans' support group that met once a week, looking for the missing pieces of our lives, and he was a stranger who walked in off the street.

He sat quietly, listening carefully, absorbing us like a sponge draws in water. Our meeting was almost over before he said his first word aside from a monosyllabic "H'lo" when he came in and sat in the corner. Once he started talking, though, you could tell he'd done a lot of thinking on his own about the situation and his part in it, and that he'd run up against the same wall we all had. We didn't know what was missing, just that it was; and that the gap it left behind was too painful to carry around with us.

There were eleven of us in the room, eleven people trying to dig through the scar tissue and find themselves a whole life to live. Aaron Robeson was a big man, and one of the blackest black men I've ever known. He had started calling himself Toke a few years back. Everybody who heard it thought it was for a "toke" of smoke, until they knew him better. With his sly, around-the-corner sense of humor, it was short for "token black." He spoke into the silence held by the stranger's twisted face, his rumbling voice shaking the air in the room like a distant B52 strike. "Did you ever cry in 'Nam, man?"

The stranger's lips were twisted and nearly blue from his effort at controlling himself. His eyes swam in a glistening pool of tears as the reply was wrenched from him. "No. Never had time, I guess."

Toke said, "That's part of what we're all missing, I think. If we couldn't cry about that crazy-stupid war, we damn-well have no idea of what to cry about. I cry now. I never know when it's going to happen, or what'll set it off." His voice softened, stroked us with emotion. "I didn't cry when my best friend's legs were blown off by a bouncin' Betty and he shot himself in the head to stop the pain; but I might cry because the sun ain't shinin' as bright as it should, or because a traffic light turns red before I get there. It don't make no sense, but there it is." True to his word, tears were running down his face. No shame showed, just an acceptance.

Jay got up and walked over to the stranger, held out his hand and said, "My name's Jay. What's yours, man?"

At first the guy didn't move, seemed to be frozen in place, then he reached out with a shaking hand and grasped Jay's in a thumbs-up grip. His left hand swept up and cupped the back side of Jay's hand like a drowning man might grab for a hand to pull him from the water. Sobs racked his body as they broke the barrier created by fifteen years of denial.

We gathered around, lending our closeness and solidarity to our new brother. Another had just taken, as had we all, the first steps to being a whole man again; the first steps toward liking himself.

Gradually, the sobs fell back, washing us with them. We gave him the room and time to gather himself together. When his voice had steadied enough, the thickness in his throat had loosened enough, he looked at us and said, "I'm Eli. At least that's what everybody calls me. My real name is Frank Willis." He hesitated, seemed to speak and hold his breath at the same time. "Could I come back again next week?"

Aaron was the loudest of us all. "If'n you don't, we'll come lookin' for you and drag your scroungy ass back here kickin' and screamin'."

The laughter felt good as we wiped the tears off our cheeks and gathered our things to leave.

I always felt better, lighter, when we left our meetings.

My Brother Says

"When I get out of here next week, me and my brother are going to start a cattle ranch up in Wyoming. We're going to buy us three, maybe four, thousand head of longhorns in Texas and drive them up to Wyoming." His hands were clasped tightly, knuckles white, in his lap and he rocked back and forth in his chair. His eyes were focused on Wyoming, not the Day Room of a VA Hospital in southern Oregon. I listened.

"George, that's my brother, he knows everything there is to know about cattle ranching. He even worked on one a couple summers back. That was before he went to jail, though." He stopped rocking and spun his head to look at me. I felt like a butterfly on a pin for a moment, then his focus slid away.

"Is George still in jail?" he asked.

I didn't know what to say. His brother's name had been Philip. Philip was dead, killed in Vietnam ten years earlier. I shrugged, he didn't notice.

"George says that there's places in Montana where the grass grows so tall you have to jump up in the air to see sunshine. We're going to get us about ten thousand acres of that grass land and raise cattle. George says you can homestead the waterholes and then nobody else can use the land. It's open range, but they can't use it if their cattle can't get to water.

"We're going to buy us five thousand head of Herefords. They're the best beef cattle you can get, you know? They'll get so fat they can hardly waddle."

He crossed his arms back across his chest, and I turned the page in the book I'd been reading. I read. He rocked. Both of us were in our own little world for thirty or forty minutes, then he stopped rocking and turned to me.

"Harry says we should move to South Dakota. You can buy land there for five dollars an acre, and we could buy us some Angus. Red ones, not them damn black ones. Best damn beef cow there ever was."

He rocked.

I read.

Have You Seen Mary?

Betty tipped her head to one side and listened as the car kicked up a spray of gravel turning into the drive. She winced when the car door slammed. Don was home, and something had him in a bad mood.

She glanced at the clock. It was five-seventeen and he was right on time. He was always on time. In nearly forty years of marriage, he'd never once come home late. At least not without calling her first. Sometimes she wished he would, just for the sake of change, for the challenge of unpredictability.

The screen door rattled as he missed the handle on the first try. She barely heard the muttered "Damn!" outside the door before it was pulled open and Don Reed shouldered his way through.

He was a stocky man, about five-nine and wearing his lightly-salted black hair short. She always told people who hadn't met him yet that he looked just like Spencer Tracy only nicer. Kind of like Tracy looked in *State of the Union*, only now he looked more like *Bad Day At Black Rock*.

Forty years of practice told her to meet his foul mood head on—to lance the boil, so to speak. "What's got you so worked up?"

"Nothing. Not a damn thing." He pulled open the door of the fridge and took out a can of beer, popping the top as he turned back to her. He looked down at the beer in his hand for a long moment, his mouth set in a hard slash. Then, with two sudden strides, he crossed to the sink and slammed the can upside-down into it.

"Not a damn thing, he says, and that's the quickest beer he's ever had." She still leaned against the counter, her arms crossed in front of her.

He glared at her, mad, but not mad at her, then grabbed a mug from the cupboard and started to pour himself a cup of coffee. "Just leave it alone, will you?"

"What is it, Don? What's wrong?"

He took a deep breath and let it and the anger seep out at the same time. He finished pouring the coffee, then turned tiredly toward her.

"I had to fire Tom Beale today." She waited patiently for it to come out. "The damn fool came in drunk again. I've told him and told him, but you just can't make some people listen. Somebody could get killed with a drunk on the floor, so I fired him—told him to pick up his pay and get the hell off the plant grounds." He said the last so quietly she could barely hear him.

She waited for him, but he looked like that was all he had to say about Tom Beale. She asked: "How was the rest of your day?"

"Griffin came down from upstairs. He said we were running about twenty-three percent ahead of our quota for the month."

"That's pretty good isn't it? I mean, you could get a bonus or something, couldn't you?"

"You know about how likely that is. These new owners aren't about to spend any money they don't have to. The only bonus I'll ever get is to be able to keep my job. Look at what happened to Harve Lansing. His production fell off a few points and he was handed an early retirement last month. No warning or nothing. He just came in on Monday morning and they told him to go home. That damn college boy took over his job. Twenty-eight years and that's all the thanks he got."

He stared out the window, lost in thought for a moment, sipping his coffee, then he asked, "Have you seen Mary?"

"Not for the last little while. She's around here somewhere, though." Betty changed the subject abruptly. "How did Tom Beale take it when you fired him?"

Don ignored the question. "How long ago did she leave?"

The corners of Betty's mouth tightened as she was shifted to the defensive. "Oh, I don't know. Maybe an hour or so. You know I don't keep that close a track on time. She'll be back for supper, though, because I told her to be here."

Don splashed the dregs of his coffee into the sink. "Her and that damn bottle of hers are probably up on the mountain again. It beats me all to hell how a daughter of mine can treat herself that way. It gets to her and everybody around her. She's got no self-respect, that's what it is..."

"You just back off that girl and leave her alone," Betty snapped. "Give her some room to get herself straightened out. She's a good girl—always has been. Now I don't want to talk about it any more. I just won't stand here and listen to you badmouth your own daughter."

Don watched her walk from the room, shoulders stiff with anger, then poured himself another cup of coffee. As he poured, he muttered under his breath, "Damn girl acts like she was in combat or something. She worked at a hospital in a base camp, for Christ's sake. She might as well have been home the whole time."

Hours later, Mary was still sitting on her hilltop, a slim figure with her elbows on her knees and her back resting against the trunk of a lonely oak. The broad valley stretched out in front of her and a restless wind sighed through the thick canopy of leaves over her head.

In her right hand, she clasped the neck of a bottle of Four Roses. It was cheap whiskey and rough as a wood rasp, but it did the job. It blurred the edges of her memories and let the warm reds and cooling purples of the setting sun shine through.

Mary knew nobody else was around. Nobody ever came up here. She was never alone anymore, though. She had a full cast of memories that followed her wherever she went. The pained cries of the wounded sounded in the trees. The rattle of death she'd heard in a hundred throats echoed in the tiny rockfall as she dribbled a handful of pebbles onto a cone-shaped pile on the ground between her legs.

These were ghosts she could live with. She'd even expected them when she volunteered for nursing duty in Vietnam.

It was the other one that got to her. He was harder to accept, more difficult to deal with. He ripped great holes in her peace of mind and left her drained of emotion and soaked with sweat. The harsh whiskey eased the pain, dulled the sense of loss she felt every time he came back to haunt her.

Mary raised the bottle and drank deeply, allowing four bursts of bubbles to rise in the amber liquid before she lowered the bottle and gasped for breath. She shuddered as it clawed its way down her throat and blossomed into white-hot fire in her stomach. She held the bottle up in the dying rays of the sun. It was half gone, and she still felt sober.

She watched the dark blue line of shadows climb the hills on the far side of the valley, tipping the bottle every time the memories came too close. The shadows were the screen on which she saw her own unending movie. Her eyes saw the past, not the advance of nightfall.

♦ ♦ ♦ ♦

He looked up—first at her face, then at her name tag. His brown eyes were drawn deep within their sockets by his pain, his focus glazed by morphine sulphate. When he spoke, the words rolled clumsily off his drug-thickened tongue. "Lieutenant Reed. What's your first name, Lieutenant?"

"Mary," she said brightly. "What's yours?" She could see it on his chart hanging on the foot of his bed, but it sometimes helped to ask, just to get them talking.

"Tom. Count the letters. That's exactly one half of Thomas." He waved at the blanket covering his mutilated body. Everything from the top of his hips down had been amputated. His skin was sewn together like a patchwork quilt, his insides held in with sutures. He'd been badly burned when he'd been hit, and was still swathed in bandages as far up as his armpits. Scar tissue, fresh and pink, traveled up the left side of his face to the top of his head. His left ear was a shapeless mass.

After three weeks in the intensive care unit, he'd been transferred into the "maybe" ward, the place where your patient "may be" there when you get back and he "may be" dead. Mary was just finishing her sixth month in the ward, four months longer than most of the nurses were able to handle.

"Do you want to talk about it? If you do, I've got the time right now." She kept her voice bright and cheerful.

"What the hell's the use of talking about it? I can talk and you can listen for as long as we want to keep the little game going, but I'll still be spending the rest of my days in bed, in pain, and doped to the gills so I can't do anything productive. There's not a damn thing you or anybody else can do to change that." His bitterness carried clearly through his drowsy voice as he fought to maintain that fine balance between the mind-numbing pain and the little death of drugged oblivion.

"How old are you, Thomas?" Mary purposely used his full name to deny his claim to being just half a man.

"Nineteen—and as old as I ever want to get."

"You've got lots of life left, Thomas. You can beat this if you really give it a try. You can come out on top. Lots of people have, you know."

"Page seventy-seven of the Army nurse's manual, huh?"

"Give me a break, will you? I just want to help."

His pupils seemed to flatten and turn opaque. "Would you make love to me, Mary?"

She stuttered, the worst thing she could have done. "I-I-I, uh, you caught me by surprise with that one, Tom. I-I don't know how to answer you. I mean, you don't have..."

He interrupted her, his voice tight with anger. "You're right. I don't have; and even if I did have, I wouldn't be able to use it because of all the drugs you pump into me. I'm nineteen goddamn years old, and I'm still a virgin. I've never even seen a naked woman in my whole life."

Tom paused and pointed at the empty expanse of bed. When he continued, he spoke softly and wearily. "As long as I look like this, I never will. And even if I did, even little Miss Mary Sunshine was quick to point out that I wouldn't be able to do anything about it."

"But there's lots of things you could do, Thomas. The whole

world is open to you." Even as she spoke, the words tasted lame in her mouth.

"The last thing I need is for you or anybody else to feel sorry for me. I just wish I was dead. I'm sure as hell not alive." He turned his head away, refusing to meet her eyes. She felt more helpless than she'd ever felt on the many other times she'd watched men die. Most of them fought for life to their last breath, never giving up, never having a chance to win.

This one was different. He actually wanted to die, in fact had nothing to live for. He well knew his own future. He would be tortured to the brink of endurance every waking moment for the rest of his life. Nothing she could do or say would change the fact that he was right. He had thought the whole thing through completely and made up his own mind. Hot tears of frustration flooded her eyes as she broke and ran from the ward.

♦ ♦ ♦ ♦

"Have you seen Mary Reed?"

The bartender looked up from the sports page quartered in his hand. "Nah, she ain't been in tonight. You might try over at Sam's. She goes there some of the time. Or maybe the bar at the hotel. If she's not there, I don't know where she would be. Getcha anything to drink?"

"Yeah, let me have a glass of whatever you have on tap." The stranger hooked a stool with his toe, pulled it over, and eased his lanky frame down onto the seat. He was about thirty, wore his faded blue jeans and sweat-stained cowboy hat like a working man, and drawled around a toothpick tucked into the corner of his mouth.

The bartender set a frosty mug of beer with a finger's width of head on it in front of the new customer, then leaned his heavy forearms on the bar. "Haven't seen you in here before. Have you known Mary long?"

The new customer lifted his mug and took a long pull before he answered, "I haven't been in here before, and it's none of your business." The stranger's eyes were a glacial gray as he met the bartender's questioning look.

The bartender's grin was wide and contagious. "It's like that with everybody who knows her, me included. People just naturally like to take care of her." He held out his big hand, "Name's Fred, what's yours?"

"Tony. Glad to meetcha." He accepted the handshake. "You always this busy?"

Fred laughed and looked ruefully around the empty room. "Not always. Sometimes it's really dead."

"How long have you known Mary?" Tony asked.

"Well, I could say it was none of your business, but I won't. We both grew up around here. I've known her all my life. I went to school with her. Hell, we even took a try at living together a couple years back. She's good people." He hesitated, looking speculatively across the bar. "I'd take it personal if somebody was to hurt that girl."

"Don't look to me for that. I owe her a big favor and just wanted to look her up and say thanks."

Fred waited for Tony to continue and he did after taking another long draw on his beer. "She saved my life in 'Nam. At least kinda. She did a favor for a buddy of mine that made me think that maybe people were all right after all. It made me fight harder to get well."

"Must've been some favor."

Tony drained his beer, set the glass on the bar, and said, "It was. Thanks for the beer." He tossed a dollar on the bar and turned to leave. He only took a couple of steps before he turned back and asked, "How do you get out to where Mary lives?"

He listened to the directions, then said, "Thanks. I think I'll try her out there first thing in the morning. It's too late now to be waking up decent people." He was out the door before Fred could say goodbye.

Mary wasn't able to sleep that night. Tom's predicament ate at her like acid. Against all her training and beliefs, she found herself agreeing with his prognosis of his life in the future. She would lie down for a few minutes, eyes squeezed tightly shut, trying to force sleep to come, then find herself up and pacing again.

Her head was whirling as she thought about how to interpret her duty. Her choices were clear. She could do as all the books and all her training told her to do and force him to hold onto a life that was no longer dear, or she could help him with the escape he so desperately wanted. It was nearly daylight when she made up her mind.

She showered quickly and left her room. Her first stop was the medical supply cupboard, where she filled a 5 cc syringe with morphine sulphate. It was four o'clock in the morning, and even a hospital like the 21st Evac in Da Nang was slowed way down. She wasn't seen as she made her way back to the "maybe" ward.

Tom was awake when she got there and had been for all the time she was gone. He was still fighting his battle against the effects of the pain-killer. She could see the shine of his eyes in the half-light of the ward as she walked up. The rest of the patients seemed to be asleep.

Mary spoke in a soft whisper, "Hi, Thomas."

"Mary. What are you doing here so late? You should've gone off shift hours ago."

"I did, but you've been bothering me."

"Yeah, sure. I've been chasing you all over the place."

"You really have. I couldn't get you off my mind. Were you serious about what you said earlier?" Her ears roared as she waited for his answer.

"You mean the part about being a virgin?"

"That, too, but mostly the part about wanting to die." Her palms were slick with sweat and she rubbed them on her hips.

"As serious as ever I could be." The bitterness that had been carried by his every word was gone.

"I can help you then." The words were hard to get out. Her heart was pounding in her chest.

His eyes opened wide, showing hope for the first time since she'd met him, maybe for the first time since he'd tripped that booby trap. "You can? I mean, will you?"

"If you really want me to. I've thought about it real hard since I talked to you earlier. I'm still not sure just what's right or wrong, but I don't think I can make that decision for you. That choice should be yours."

"Do it!" he hissed at her. "For God's sake, do it! Let me get out of here while I still like who I am."

"I think I figured out the best way to do it. Maybe it will help you with all your problems at the same time."

"I trust you, Mary. Do what you think's best."

Tears rolled down her cheeks as she lifted the syringe from her pocket and laid it gently on the blanket at the empty foot of the bed. She moved slowly, unbuttoning her blouse, shrugging it off, and laying it neatly beside the syringe. The rest of her clothes followed, piece by piece.

When she finally stood nude before the astonished Thomas, she gently lifted his hand, placed it on her breast, then slowly guided it down her warm flank and across the swell of her hip. She reached across and grasped his other hand, drawing it to her, murmuring encouragement as he began to explore her body on his own. Gently, with a touch as light as a feather, she stroked his forehead, the side of his neck, and across his shoulder.

His fearful fingers quested and found her warmth as she leaned forward to kiss him full on the mouth. His response was tentative at first, then grew stronger. She waited until his arms encircled her, drew her to him, then asked: "Do you still want to die?"

He met her gaze levelly. "Stay with me as I go. I don't want to be alone, I just don't want to ever hurt again."

Tom's eyes were wide as he caressed her warm, soft skin. He hardly paid attention as Mary fed the morphine sulphate into his IV tube. It was his first time ever to caress a woman's flesh, and the drug heightened his senses for several long, glorious moments before dropping him into the oblivion he sought. He died painlessly, carrying the wonder of the moment with him. Mary stayed, holding him lovingly in her arms until she was sure he was gone.

Mary was still crying as she drew her clothing back on, then she picked up the hypo and cast about to see if she'd left any evidence of her act. She saw none and was turning to leave when a softly-drawled voice spoke to her from the darkness.

"That was my best friend, lady. I think what you did was a mighty good thing. Thank you, from Thomas."

A sob broke from Mary's lips as she fled the room. She met

no objections when she requested a change of ward the following morning, and never saw the man who'd spoken to her from the darkness.

♦ ♦ ♦ ♦

The sudden crash of breaking glass woke Don Reed at three-thirty in the morning. He got up and looked out the window. Below, his daughter lay sprawled across the sidewalk where she'd fallen. He cursed softly all the way down the stairs and out the front door.

The empty Four Roses bottle lay broken on the sidewalk, light glistening off the sharp edges. Mary's hair was disheveled, her clothing mussed. She was coated with mud to both knees and up her left side where she'd fallen in the creek while trying to make it home in the dark. He gathered her tenderly into his arms and carried her inside the house and to her room.

Betty met him in the hallway, wringing her hands nervously, fearful of an angry explosion from her often volatile husband. "Is she all right?"

"Looks like she's just cold, wet, muddy, and drunk. Let's get her put to bed." He carried Mary into her room and placed her gently on the floor. He backed out of the room, embarrassedly letting Betty take over from there.

A few minutes later, Betty came out of Mary's room and found her husband sitting on the couch, in the dark, with his face buried in his hands. She sat down next to him and looped an arm around his shoulders, pulling him closer to her. They sat quietly for a bit, then he said in a choked voice, "I'm going to call Tom Beale in the morning and give him his job back."

Conversation in a Bathroom

"I heard you could get a woman for all night and it only cost you a dollar...and you could get a whole duffle bag full of pot for ten bucks." He was young, and his voice was raised excitedly. He'd heard right, but he didn't know the rest of the story. He knew the legends, but he didn't know about seeing the eyes of an eighty-year-old man peering out at the world from the face of a nineteen-year-old boy.

I looked him over carefully. Freckles across the bridge of his nose, tobacco tucked firmly into his right cheek, and wearing a John Wayne swagger like a badge. I tried to see deep inside him. As usual, it didn't work. I tried to tell whether it would do either of us any good for him to know what it was like in an undeclared war like Vietnam.

I shook my head sadly and turned from him. It'd be a waste of time. I'd say something about the feeling of warm blood splashing over your face and the rapid, panicked search to find out if it was yours. He'd hear about glory and ticker-tape parades. There was nothing I could teach him. I was tired of trying to teach the innocent about the loss of innocence. It was an uphill battle at best, with nothing to be gained.

"Where ya goin'?" His voice still carried that high-pitched

whine of beer and glory-lust. I got two more steps before his hand fell on my shoulder.

I turned to face him, looked down at his hand until it fell away into embarrassment. "To the can." I made my way through the press of people to the bathroom, feeling the claustrophobic constriction of the crowd. I'd chosen this place because I knew nobody here and wouldn't have to talk to anybody. I wasn't in the mood tonight. But somehow, out of all the people in the crowd, he had attached himself to me and struck up a conversation.

I closed the bathroom door behind me, turned on the cold water and splashed my face with it, once, twice, then in a flurry. Water flew in all directions, my shirtsleeves became soaked.

The door behind me opened again, and the kid followed me into the room. I grabbed a towel off the rack and buried my face in it. "I'm joining the Marines next week." The pride in his voice caused the bile to rise in my throat. I looked up, curious to see what his face showed. His chin was up, chest and jaw thrust out, stomach pulled tight. He was as complete a picture of ignorance and belligerence as I had ever seen.

The fear was there, too. I could smell it on him like old urine. He wanted so much to be right, and was so afraid of being wrong.

I wanted to be wrong as much as he wanted to be right, but everybody dies a little in a war. Everybody loses a little piece of themselves that they can never get back. I'd lost my piece over fifteen years before, and spent nearly the whole time since trying to find out what was missing and how to go about finding it again. Then I figured out that it was gone forever and it was up to me to live without it.

"They told me that I might get to go to Lebanon or one of those other places. I figure to smell me some gunpowder." The challenge in his eyes was as much to himself as it was to me. He wasn't sure enough to just do it, he wanted somebody to tell him it was all right, that he would be a hero.

"Have you ever seen a dead man?"

He faltered, his chin drooped the tiniest fraction. There was a flicker of discomfort far back in his eyes. "No. But I know I could handle it."

"What can you handle? Can you handle seeing him through a pair of binoculars? How about laying in a ditch by the side of

Conversation in a Bathroom

the road all burnt and twisted? Is that what you can handle? What if it's your best friend laying on top of you, staring you in the face with glazed-over eyes when you wake up and you realize that you are at the bottom of a pile of dead men and everybody thinks you're dead, too? Which one? Where do you stop being able to handle it?"

He walked over to the urinal, unbuttoning the fly on his pants. He needed to do something to cover up the uncertainty he was feeling. He waited until he was done before he answered. "I think I can handle it OK. Other people did and made it through, so why shouldn't I?"

"That's not the question you need to ask yourself. You need to know 'Why should I?' That's the important one." I turned and walked from the room. My eyes were blurry and refused to focus, my pulse hammered in my throat.

This time, he didn't follow me.

Devil's Dance

I woke up, the sheets soaking with my own sweat and the terror of the night still making my heart pound loudly in my ears. It was always so real, so vivid. I didn't just dream like everybody else, I relived the whole damn thing. I didn't just see it and hear it—I could feel it—I could taste it—I could smell it. The images were still running before my eyes, and would keep on showing the whole horrible movie until I turned on the bedside lamp and whited them out.

The click of the lamp switch was loud in the stillness of the night. It always sounded like the hammer of a .45 being drawn back. That's where it really started. At least that's where it started for me.

I gathered a blanket around me and walked tiredly into the living room. The house was quiet as I settled into the recliner and scooped up the remote control. It didn't matter what was on, I just needed to have somebody there with me. That's what the headshrinkers said, anyway.

It was Fred Astaire. I was so sick and tired of seeing fluffy late night movies. I dropped the remote back onto the end table and pulled the blanket tighter, hoping the ghosts would leave me alone this time. Sometimes they did...most times they didn't. The night was all they had left, and they didn't like to waste their time by letting me get off easy.

Little Fred, his feet as light as dandelion fuzz, tapped his way across the stage. The staccato rhythm made my fists clench and I could feel my nails biting into the palms of my hands. I didn't figure they'd bleed again. The skin was a mass of scar tissue from years of such damage.

Sweat broke out on my forehead as the machine gun rhythm of his feet dragged me back into the jungle with my eyes open. I saw an old man panic and run into a hail of bullets, saw him cut nearly in half by the barrage, felt the butt of the automatic rifle rap out its rhythm against my shoulder. I heard, again, the crashing silence that followed.

"It was a war. I was a soldier in a war. He was an enemy." I said this out loud, over and over. It was my litany, my incantation to drive the devils out of my head, out of my dreams. Sometimes it worked. This time I just sweated more and waited for the rest of the devils to come for me. Tonight we would dance together, know each other. I could tell already that I had slept my last for this night.

I forced the image from my mind, exorcised the old man just as I'd done so many times before. I fought. I sat there in my own chair, in my own living room, and I fought for my sanity. I fought to keep them away from me.

The memory of the click of the light switch came back to haunt me. I could feel the muzzle of the .45 pressing against the hollow behind my ear, cold and impersonal. No, not impersonal. Impending death is always personal, no matter who you are or how much you'd welcome it.

I could hear Sergeant Agouter's voice hissing in my ear, "You get up there, boy. You get up there and you hold up your end of the stick, or I'm just going to have to blow your pointy little head off."

I believed him. I still do. He would have killed me and blamed it on the VC without another thought. He was the most cold-blooded bastard I've ever met.

I picked up my rifle and moved into the center of the village. I never even knew the name of the town. It was in section Charlie Sixteen, and we were running a search and destroy. We'd run others before, and I'm sure there were others after. It was a war, you know.

The villagers were lined up against the wall of the central hut. They were scared, anybody could see that. Pamphlets were still scattered on the ground, so we knew they'd been notified of the mission. They'd been told—in Thai, Vietnamese, English and Cambodian—to clear the area, and that any people still in the area when we arrived would be considered VC.

They were still there. By the rules we'd invented, that made them VC; but this was just a little podunk village. These people were no more VC than I was. I looked over my shoulder and looked at the Sarge. He was staring at me, his hand resting on the butt of his .45.

I turned back, raised my M-16 and opened fire on the villagers. The rest of the squad fired at the same time. They fell like grain before a scythe. I could see them yelling, see them trying to run, but I couldn't hear them over the roaring in my own ears. That waited until much later, years later. Then I could hear them just fine.

Back in my living room, sweat was running in a torrent down my chest and back. My face was beaded with it, it dripped from my chin. My fists were clenched in helpless rage as I watched myself reload and fire again. I was still screaming and yanking on the trigger when the palm of Sarge's hand cracked against the side of my face.

The villagers were dead, all seventeen of them. Shot to doll rags by a gaggle of stupid boys led and driven by a sadistic asshole.

Fred was talking soft and soothingly to a pretty young thing who was crying for some reason or another. She cried and cried. Tears ran from my own eyes, mingling with the rivers of sweat coursing down my body.

I tensed myself. I knew what would happen next. It always did. As soon as the right sound set it off, I would be back in my own hell. Fred's girl did it this time. Suddenly her hand flashed up and slapped him across the face. The smack was loud in the stillness, and his face bore an expression of surprise.

I kicked the Sarge's chair out from under him, yanking the .45 from his holster as he fell. He was surprised, too. He was even more surprised as the first bullet took him in the belly. The other NCOs that had been sitting at the poker table with him scattered like quail. They didn't matter, so I paid them no attention.

The .45 kicked in my hand again and again, driving Agouter down into the floor. I could feel the tears on my cheek, hot and wet. I could feel the .45 in my hand, kicking the life out of that animal. Then the whole world seemed to fall in on me.

Somehow, one of the other NCOs got around to my side and grabbed my gun hand. Another drove a series of punches into my stomach. When the pistol was pulled from my hand, it was quickly reversed and the muzzle was pushed against my ear. The snap of the hammer as the trigger was pulled on an empty chamber was harsh.

It was the last sound I registered for a year-and-a-half. When I did wake up, I didn't know my own name. I didn't remember anything of my past. All that came back later.

The doctors said this was progress.

A Penny for Your Thoughts

"A penny for your thoughts." Karen Fuller was a plump and pleasant sixty, gray and lined with the years. Her voice was always firm with her convictions, always soft with her cares.

"Not worth a penny and I can't make change, dear." Chester was as spare as Karen was plump, wore a thick mustache over a bare chin, and had been married to Karen since she was nineteen and he was twenty-six. It was a long time, and he couldn't imagine a world without her in it. Not a day went by without him telling her how much he loved her. They both valued their relationship more than anything else in the world, and both accepted the other as the person they were.

"Somethin's botherin' you. You got so quiet I thought you were asleep for a while there."

"Just thinkin' 'bout the boys. They been layin' heavy on me lately."

"Is there somethin' you haven't told me?"

He was long in answering. "Just wonderin' where I went wrong."

She pulled the straight-back chair over by the rocker he was sitting in, scooped up his hand and pulled it to her chest. The afternoon light coming in through the window caught and gleamed off the tears in the corners of her eyes. "Chester, you just forget thinkin' like that. You did good by them boys. It ain't your fault they're like they are."

"Maybe...maybe if I'd done somethin' different. Maybe if I'd spent more time with them. Oh, I don't know. I just wish we'd hear from them once in a while. I keep wonderin' if they're alive or dead."

"We hear from Frank ever' once in a while."

"Last time was near two years ago, and he wanted to borrow some money so he and his boyfriend could buy themselves a house. It's been ten for Russell. I just can't think of what I could've done different."

"You're a good husband, Chester, and a good father, too. They made up their own minds about how to live and followed through on it."

"Every man should leave his mark on the land. I guess mine's goin' to be a queer and a deserter from the Army."

Karen slapped his hand gently. "You just hush up. Your bitin' at yourself ain't goin' to change a single thing. We raised those boys to make up their own minds and not lean on anybody for support. We got no reason to get upset if they did it."

"I'm goin' to turn sixty-seven next week and I want to see those boys before I die. I want to tell 'em I love 'em. I want them to know I care."

"They know that, and they care, too. They're just as stiff-necked as you are, though." She was interrupted by the ringing of the telephone. "You put a smile on your face before I get back here, now. You hear me, Chester?"

He patted her on her ample rear as she walked by. "I hear you, babe, I hear you."

"Hello."

"Momma, this is Russ. Could I talk to Dad, please? I want to tell him happy birthday."

The Fishing Trip

"It's the only time I'm really comfortable, you know what I mean?" The sun was still just a silvery pink promise beyond the eastern horizon, and the two men just darker puddles of shadow in the stillness of the pre-dawn morning. The warm scent of coffee mixed with the cool pine and the soft-edged, over-ripe scent of cottonwoods. They spoke quietly, not wanting to disturb the hushed sense of timelessness that surrounded them.

"Stan, look at it. You're thirty-six-years-old, married, you got two kids, and you just quit your job for the third time this year. The world is not just one great big fishing hole, no matter how much you'd like it to be. When are you going to grow up and face your responsibilities?"

"When am I going to grow up? What about you, little brother. You've been on the same job for ten years, and you hate it. You pulled the wool over the draft board's eyes with some cock-and-bull story about needing to take care of Mom, so you wouldn't have to go to war and fight like a man. You brown-nose your way through every single day of your life. You're in debt to the American Dream so far that you'll never get out. And to top off that glorious story, you think you're happy." He drained the cup and tossed the grounds out onto the carpet of pine needles.

"I am happy. I have most of the things I want, and I'm getting around to those that I don't have. So what if my job is a bummer, that's only eight hours of my life and it's not enough to bother me. I won't let it. It gives me the money I want to get what I want."

"That's the difference, I guess. You want things, and I want the wind at my back. You want to own, and I want to see it all as I pass by. You want a position in the community and I want a view of the universe. We just want different things."

"What's Mary Alice want?"

"She wants what I want. We're two of a kind."

"I don't know just how to break this to you, brother mine, but she asked me for some money yesterday. She said she was going to file for a divorce." He paused, then said flatly, "I let her have it."

"How much was it? I'll pay you back as soon as I can."

"Is that all you can say? Don't you even give a damn that your wife borrowed money from your brother so she could divorce you?"

The wind sang in the tall trees while the waves lapped at the shore of the small lake. These were the only sounds for several long moments. "Are you even going to talk to me? I'm your brother, for God's sake, talk to me."

When he did speak, his voice rasped like two dead sticks rubbed together. "What's there to say. She wants out, let her go. I'm not going to keep her a prisoner against her will."

"A prisoner! Damn it, Stan, she loves you. She'd stay with you and make it work if you'd just meet her halfway. You haven't given her a chance to really make it work."

"She doesn't love me. She loves a picture of me that doesn't exist. She loves the me she built in her brain. If I'm not like that, it's because she built the picture wrong, not because I haven't given her a chance. I did all the changing I'm going to do in the year-and-a-half I was in 'Nam. I'm not going to try to become somebody else just because she or anybody else wants me to. I'm me, and I like it that way."

The sky was enough lighter that Fred could just see the shade of his brother stand up, pick up his fishing pole, and fade silently into the surrounding darkness.

After a moment, Fred poured himself another half-cup of coffee and settled back to wait for enough light to see well. He couldn't see in the dark like his brother could.

Ticker Tape

"A war ain't nothin' but a war." The old man sighted along the stick and stroked the cue ball. The three-bank shot eased around the table and slipped gently into the target pocket. He twisted the chalk onto the tip with a squeak, and leaned into his next shot. As he stroked the ball in, he said, "You kin die a thousand different ways, but the worms get you all the same. In the long run, all that matters is that you have pride in your part of it, know you did your job well."

We had the argument every time we got together. We butted our heads, talked ourselves blue, and got nowhere. He'd been to war, killed men, and been hit a few times himself, but there was a difference I couldn't find the words to show him, and it was important to me that he understand.

"Grandpa, there's a difference. I don't know how to say it, but there is a difference. Vietnam is the only war we ever lost."

He interrupted me. "It don't matter if you won or lost. It just matters that you gave it your best. You did do that, didn't you?"

"Maybe that's a part of the difference. We weren't allowed to give our best. They had rules against it. You gave just as much as there was room for, and you swallowed the rest—or hid it in a fog of smoke."

He missed his shot and I moved up to the table for mine. He was a finesse shooter, and I was a banger, but for all that, I could almost hold my own with him. I had a two-fer sitting at the far end of the table, and slapped it down without even taking serious aim. They both went, but I left myself bad and missed the following shot.

While he was chalking up for the next shot, he grinned at me. "Knew you'd do it that way. Cost you the game, just like it always does." He was right. He ran the rest of his balls and sank the eight ball handily. That gave him three games to my one.

"What'd you bring with you when you left that war, boy?"

"A duffel bag of clothes and..."

"Use your head for something other than keeping your ears from running together ever' time you take a breath. What do you remember most about that place?" He laid his stick on the table, took mine out of my hand and did the same thing, then led me over to the bar.

I thought about his question while we waited for the drinks to get there. After I'd had a sip, I started talking and he started listening.

"It was hot when I got there, and got hotter all the time. It rained five months out of the year. The beach was white sand, and the water warm. The only thing you could get to drink that was cold had booze in it."

"You're dancin' instead of talkin'. Get to the point. What do you want to tell me that you haven't already told me? What's going to make me change my mind about what went on over there?"

"I don't know, Grandpa. If I could figure that out, I would've told you already. I just wish I could tell you what it was like over there without it feeling like I was trying to get a reaction out of you, trying to con you into thinkin' that I did somethin' special."

"Maybe you're trying to get a reaction out of me, and maybe not. It really don't matter. What does matter is this. You need to come to terms with what happened over there before anybody else can."

"Nobody else wants to. They all want to bury it under the rug instead of taking a good look at it. It hurts to look at it, hurts all of us, whether we were there or not. People don't usually go out and look for something that is going to hurt them."

Ticker Tape

He leveled his piercing gray eyes at me, peering out from under his bushy white eyebrows. The lines of his face deepened, and he said: "Is that what you're doin'? Are you afraid to look at what happened over there? Are you scared of yourself, of what you'll see?"

He made me mad when he talked to me like this.

"No!" I snapped at him. "I remember all of what happened over there. I remember how the newspapers painted the picture. I remember what it was like when I came back."

"What was it like over there?"

"I was a scared kid ten thousand miles from home fighting against other scared kids who had no more real idea of just what the hell was goin' on than I did."

"That's a pretty fair description of war, if you ask me. It's been just like that for all the years I've been around."

"You frustrate the hell out of me, Grandpa, do you know that?"

"Can't. You're too busy doin' it to yourself. Ain't no room for somebody else to do it. Thing is, though, you haven't really showed me a thing that was different about this war. Sounds the same for you as it was for me when I fought in Europe. People died. Memories changed to fill the gaps. You shit blood every time somebody fired a gun. Yep, sounds the same to me."

"Bullshit!" I was mad as hell now. "You came back to ticker tape parades. People believed in what you did. Nobody called you a 'baby-killer.' It *was* different. Your family met the ship. People threw confetti and cheered. I took a cab from the airport."

"Is that what's different, then? What other people think? I thought you were a big boy who did his own thinkin' and followed up on what he came up with."

"Damn right I do! And I think we got a raw deal. We got screwed every way there was—by the press, by business, by the very people we fought to protect."

"Ain't sayin' you didn't. What'd you do about it?"

"What do you mean?"

"We came back to ticker tape parades and screaming fans, alright. We felt real good about that. But we also came back to our girlfriends living with other men, jobs non-existent or taken by them what stayed behind. You got a Veterans' Administration, don't you? We didn't have that."

I hadn't thought of it in that way.

"We had to fight another war at home, just like you boys have to do. We had to get recognized and fight as a unit, just like you boys have to do. Ain't no difference. You ain't nothing but a tool rustin' in the shed until you get up off your duffs and do somethin' about it."

It bore some thinking. I set about doing that while Grandpa went and started putting away our cues. When he got back, there was a twinkle in his eye.

"Good to see my grandson startin' to grow up. You keep thinkin', start doin', and you'll have that ticker tape parade, yet." He clapped me on the shoulder and we went out into the afternoon sunshine together.

Western Union

Trish had heard the doorbell ring, and the heavy footsteps and rustle of the morning newspaper as her husband, Dave, went to answer the door. The murmur of voices barely reached into the kitchen where she was putting together breakfast. Then the front door closed softly, only the click of the latch carrying through the hallway. No footsteps, no following sound at all.

Curious, she grabbed a towel off the rack and went to check on him, craning her neck to see around the corner. He was standing by the closed front door, still staring at it, motionless.

"Dave. Who was it, honey?"

Dave turned to her, face gray, looking eighty instead of fifty. He waved a crumpled yellow piece of paper in a small circle, moved his mouth in strange fish-like motions without any sound escaping. She looked at the paper, saw the familiar black Western Union logo across the top.

Dave looked so stricken, so shocked by what he had read. She suddenly knew beyond a doubt what message was on the paper. "It's Ben, isn't it? Ben's dead." Her voice broke into a croak, and Dave waddled to meet her, scoop her into his arms. He couldn't speak, only nod his head and swab helplessly at his wife's sudden flood of tears.

Sobs racked her body as she helplessly succumbed to the grief. Dave stood stoically, stroking her hair as she twitched and jerked against him. He felt the front of his shirt gather her tears and hold them against his chest. He pulled her closer and closer, tighter and tighter, his massive arms crushing her tenderly to him.

But he was too stunned by the news, too forced by his wife's need to give in to the pain he felt. That, he knew, would come later. He, too, would have his moment of terrible mind-numbing grief, but it would have to wait until he had taken care of his wife. Until then, he felt removed, on the outside of the most important happening in his life looking in.

Gradually, the sobs wore down. The first burst of pain washed past. The sobs wore from an all-encompassing, soul-crushing stab to a dull and empty ache; a feeling of loss.

When Trish had her emotions more under control, she backed away from him, wiped her eyes with the backs of her hands, and said, "I got breakfast burnin' in the kitchen." She hurried off, embarrassed by the extra emotional load she had put on her husband.

Dave stood there for a minute more, then went back to his recliner and sat down. He picked up the phone and called work. It was answered on the third ring. "Paula, this is Dave. I won't be in for a couple of days. Get somebody to cover for me." He hung up without waiting for an answer and stared unseeingly at the blank tube of the TV.

Trish came in from the kitchen and sat down on the couch across from him. "What're we going to do?"

"Do about what?" Mandy was short for Amanda, and she had just turned seventeen the week before. She rounded the corner, her face lit with the smile she started every day with and skidded to a stop. The stricken expression on both her parents' faces told her that something terrible had happened.

"Come here, honey." Dave drew Mandy into his arms, stroking her dark brown hair back from her eyes, searching for the right words to tell the girl about her big brother.

"What's wrong?" she demanded. Her voice rose shrilly, the fingers of her left hand dug into her father's shoulder. "Tell me! You're scaring me!"

Trish jumped from the couch and gathered the now-panicked

girl into her arms. "There, there, honey," she soothed, "Everything's going to be all right."

Mandy wrenched from her mother's grip. "*What's* going to be all right?"

Her father's voice cut through her panic, used up—dead. "It's Ben, cupcake. He...he's dead."

Her hand flashed out, smacked loudly against his cheek, left a reddening mark on his cheek. "You're lying! Tell me you're lying!"

He shook his head sadly, ignoring her outburst. "No honey, it's true. We just got the telegram."

She cried, "I don't believe it! I won't believe it!" and ran from the room. Trish followed her, trying to reason with her at every step up the stairs. Dave listened as they faded from hearing behind the slam of Mandy's bedroom door, then opened the telegram again and read the words over slowly. "WE REGRET TO INFORM YOU THAT YOUR SON, PFC. BENJAMIN CROFT, WAS KILLED IN ACTION ON 11/19/72. PLEASE ACCEPT OUR CONDOLENCES."

He carefully folded the thin paper into a neat square, then let his hands fall to his lap. For a long moment, he stared blankly across the room. Then his face slowly folded and creased, his eyes filled with tears, and he said in a shaky voice: "My God, Ben, what have we done to you?"

You Know I Do

Her voice cut through the dark.
Ice cold.
Razor sharp.
"He's your son!"
She was right about that. He looks just like me. My smile. My eyes. He even walks just like me.
"I know that."
"Then why won't you even hold him?"
There wasn't anything I could say about that, either. I knew all the reasons why I should have shown the love I felt for David. I knew them all, and they were all good. Good for somebody. Good for just about anybody.
Not for me.
"I don't know."
The words slipped hoarsely from my lips into the darkness and cowered in the deepest pools of shadows.
"Don't you love him?"
"You know I do."
"Do I? *He* damn well don't."
I gathered the darkness around me like a shroud. "I do."

"Well, damn it, why won't you show him? He loves you more than he loves the way the sun shines. Why won't you show him?"

I could feel it rising in my throat. It tasted bad before I even said it.

"Get off my ass! He knows it, just like you know it. I wouldn't be here if I didn't love him."

"You're not here, you son-of-a-bitch. Sure, your body is here, but you don't give a damn thing of yourself. You are just as far away as the damn moon."

"Shit!"

"Yeah, that's about what you put into this thing, shit."

"Go to hell!"

"Get out of my face. Just leave me alone and get out of my face."

"Look at you! Look at us. We ain't gettin' nowhere. You just sit flat on your ass and I try to make a family. I love you. I love David. I love the both of you, and I can't stand to see you pull back like you do."

"There ain't a damn thing I can do about it. I try. I try so hard I shake and sweat with the effort. I try over and over, but I can't break the pattern. It's like there's something dead in me. I just wish I knew what the hell to do."

"You can show your son that you care."

"You make it sound easy."

"That's just how it is."

"Sure."

"I mean it. All you have to do is show him a little of the affection you say you feel. That's all. That's the whole thing. All you have to do is show him you care."

When a muscle gets so tired it shivers and shakes, your face will give you away. My cheeks bunched and twisted while I tried to form the words. Finally they squeezed their way out.

"I can't."

"What?"

"Forget it."

"No, really. What did you say? I couldn't hear you."

"Forget it."

"Not a chance."

She couldn't see my tears in the dark. She couldn't feel my

hands shake. She didn't know about the small dead body—so still in the yellow dust of Vietnam. The horrible mistake of a scared kid firing at a noise in the dark. The numbing fear of ever hurting another kid.

"I'm here."

"I know you are."

"No, I really mean it. I'm here for you. I'm here to be on your side."

"I don't have a side."

"You've got more sides than anybody I've ever known."

I couldn't think of anything I could say to that, so I was quiet.

"Why won't you let us in?"

I let the darkness answer for me.

"Talk to me."

"And tell you what?"

"Tell me why you won't let your son know you love him."

"I want to go to sleep now."

"So do it. Why should I care?"

"Good night."

"Tell him, not me. He's the one who really needs you."

"You don't need me?"

"Don't twist my words."

"I didn't."

"Bull."

"What do you want me to say?"

"Do you love your son?"

I took a deep breath and let it out slowly. "You know I do."

"I don't know any such thing. You tell me one thing and I see another."

"I love you. I love David. I love the both of you."

"Show me."

"You're not from Missouri."

"Show me."

You stick your fork into a plate of spaghetti and twist it. When you have it twisted tight on the tines of your fork, you slide it into your mouth. I felt twisted tight by the love I felt. I felt tighter because they would never know just how much I really cared.

"Show me!" she demanded.

I let the force of her careen off the dome of my protection.

She sat up in our bed, the palm of her hand ringing off my cheek. "He's your son!"

I don't know what happened. One minute I was laying there in the dark and the next the room reverberated with the echo of her blow.

"Don't you feel anything? Are you just going to sit there and do nothing?"

"What do you want me to do?"

"Love your son." She said it simply, like it was the easiest thing in the world.

"I do."

"Show him. He needs you."

"I need the both of you."

"Bull. You don't need a thing."

"I don't want to lose you."

"You can't lose what you don't have."

"What do you mean by that crack?"

"Just that. If you don't put anything into it, you don't have anything. That's just the way it is."

"I can't lose you, neither of you."

She was real quiet in the soft darkness. The seconds dragged into minutes, minutes into hours. The soft intrusion of daylight swept the problem into a pile in the corner. When I was in the shower, she said, "David wants to come into the shower with you."

I shoved the curtain back and scooped David into my arms. I squeezed him tight while he hung in my wet arms. I kissed him and pulled him tighter against my chest.

"I love you, son."

"I know that."

The Professor

Somebody said his name was Herman Molanski, but I don't know. He was known as "the Professor" by everybody who knew him. A thick shock of blue-black hair and bushy eyebrows topped a frame that would have looked more at home stretched between the weights lifted by Alexi Alexiev. He had no more contours to his frame than a steel bar, and no more give to his personality.

His greatest fault, if you could call it that, was a complete and total recall. Not just that like a photographic memory, but for every detail of everything that had ever happened around him. He never lost an argument, because he could call up the precise page of information of the precise volume and quote it without flaw.

His greatest saving grace was quite probably his tremendous love of the works of both William Shakespeare and Jim Beam. They had a humanizing effect on this memory machine that had to be seen to be appreciated.

A lonely individual by choice, he was not yet twenty-three when he arrived in Da Nang and kept mostly to himself. He drank to enjoy his own company, and that of his two greatest friends, "Bill and Jim" as he called them. People left him alone more for his sharp attacks than because of his abrasive personality. In the time that was the Vietnam war, all of us were abrasive to an extent, and all of us needed the company of other human beings to soften the blow.

Almost every evening, halfway through a fifth of Jim Beam, the Professor would tip his stolen straight-back wooden chair back against the wall of the barracks and close his eyes. His black-rimmed glasses would slip down his beak of a nose and he would begin to speak.

We all listened, but it was a heaven to me. I had read, but I had never learned to love the work of the long-dead "Bill." It had never come alive in front of me, breathed the air I was breathing, moved before my eyes. The thump of his chair against the wall was a call to glory for me, a call I never missed if I could help it.

His voice changed with each of the parts, now strong and dominating, now weak and subservient; male and female came alive in the room. The characters from so long ago, exhumed from the dusty pages of the past, pranced and strutted in all their glory.

With his voice alone, he could carry us to the bleakness of Denmark, or the glory that was Italy. He could flaunt the tomfoolery of a man with the head of an ass, or make us feel what it was like to go through life with a humped back.

On occasion, as rare as could be arranged, somebody dared to interrupt the Professor during his visit with his friends. When that happened, the front legs of his chair would settle to the floor with a bump, his eyes would open slowly, a forefinger would push his glasses back up his nose, and he would speak slowly and clearly to the offender. Always, the reaction was the same. One of his poetic recriminations has stuck in my thoughts over the years.

"May the bleeding piles assail you from your head down to your feet. May crabs the size of lobsters crawl on your balls and eat. And when you're old and withered, and a syphilitic wreck, may you fall down through your asshole and break your fuckin' neck."

Sometimes they were just short one-liners, and sometimes they were half-a-hundred lines of vituperation. Always, they were effective, and always they fit the victims of his counterattack.

When he had finished what he had to say, he would tip his

chair back against the wall again, take a long pull on his bottle of whiskey, and start up again precisely where he'd left off.

As the years have passed since, I find I envy the Professor more and more. Unlike the rest of us, he carried a real and vivid world with him wherever he went. He dealt with the reality that was a war only at times he felt strong enough to ensure personal preservation. His scars—and we *all* carry them—are scattered in the ashes of the past and will be exhumed only at times he chooses.

I Hate John Wayne

He died right there in front of me.

I stood with my back squeezed against the wall to let the gurney through—jostled by the half-dozen medics surrounding it.

"We're losing him!"

"Christ! Do something!"

"Let me in there—get the fuck out of my way!"

"Look out for the tube, you'll yank the needle out of his arm."

"Won't make no difference. The sucker's dead."

"He's not dead until I say he is."

"Who the hell do you think you are, God?"

"Shut up. You can either help or get out of the damn way."

"Fuck you."

"He didn't have a chance. Never did. What a stupid fuckin' stunt."

"He's dead."

"Thank you, God. Can we go get a cup of coffee now?"

"Don't you feel anything?"

"Not any more."

"Look at him. Kids like him shouldn't die like this."

They pushed the cart past me, the eighteen-year-old laying

dead on his front side, his stomach blown out the middle of his back. He'd dived on a grenade instead of away from it.

The last thing I heard as they rounded the corner was, "I hate John Wayne. It's all his fuckin' fault."

Something to Live With

I saw him again, a face floating in the crowd of returning soldiers at the Ft. Lewis, Washington In-Processing Depot. His face was deeply tanned and lined with experience and harsh weather rather than time. His blue eyes, so pale they seemed to fade into the surrounding white, captured my glance. They impaled me, searched me for purpose, then he melded magically into the surging crowd. I felt a cold ripple of fear racing up my spine. My palms were wet and slippery with sweat. I had memories, too.

In a near-panic, I pushed through the crowd, across the current of humanity to the comparative safety of a cinder block wall. I tossed my duffle bag down and swung my back against the cool comfort. I wanted no part of him, not now and not then.

The crowd faded and I was once again on that bus in Da Nang, headed for the Monkey Mountain PX. There were only a few of us on the trip. Thursday afternoons were a slow time for business.

Across the aisle from me and two seats back sat two kids. I was twenty, but they were kids. One was drunk and bragging; I remember him most. He had a big gap between his front teeth, and the camouflage cover for his helmet was faded by the sun.

That didn't mean much, though, he could have bought it or stolen it from a real salt.

The M-16 in his hands carried a light coating of brown dust, the brown from the interior, not the yellow of the coast. He laughed a lot, trying to sound like he was a hardtail, but he didn't know the difference between bravery and bravado. He hit the bottle about every third sentence.

His partner was quieter and darker, and drank fearfully when the bottle was handed to him. He was a newbie. I could see the fold marks on his fatigues that were still dark green instead of the sun-faded, almost-khaki they would become if he lived long enough. He even smelled new, that fear smell that lingers until you learn enough to stay alive.

The bottle gurgled again. The gap-toothed kid's voice was louder. "I wasted 'em right where they stood. Burned 'em down. Turned out they wasn't VC, just wanted to get something to eat, but what the fuck, over? We didn't know." He drank deeply from his bottle, then wiped his mouth with the back of his sleeve and chuckled. "They was an old lady and a little girl, maybe three or four years old. You should've seen 'em twitchin' and dancin' when those bullets slammed into 'em. I had my magazine clear full of tracers, eighteen hot mother-fuckers. Set their clothes on fire."

He laughed again and took another drink of the raw whiskey. "Boy, there ain't nothin' stinks like a gook on fire."

The new guy took the offered bottle and drank deeply, choking on the combination of raw whiskey and what he'd just heard. He'd been expecting glamour, maybe, but what he got was the dirty end of the stick.

A man stirred in the seat behind them. He had a way of blending in, so I hadn't noticed him before. He lifted the front of his bush hat with his right forefinger and uncurled from his sleeping position. I could tell he'd been around awhile from the tan on his face and arms that was darker than his faded fatigues. He looked up, saw me looking at him, and winked one of his nearly colorless eyes.

I can't really say I saw what happened next. I mean, I was looking right at him and all, but I just didn't really see how he did it. He started to move, his long arms reached over the back of the seat. I heard a snapping sound, heard it easily over the sound of the grinding motor, then the kid's head was laying on his chest at an odd angle.

It was over before it began. The kid who'd been bragging about killing two innocent people was dead and the other kid didn't even notice. He just tucked his chin deeper into his chest and took another swallow from the bottle, grateful for his partner's new silence.

The big guy got up from his seat and stepped out the door of the still-moving bus. I threw a glance over my shoulder at the dead kid and followed the salt out while the bus driver was still yelling about rules and regulations. It was rules and regulations I was worried about. I sure as hell didn't want to get involved in an inquiry over a dead kid with a broken neck.

I hit the road running to avoid falling, kicking up little puffs of yellow dust. As I slowed to a stop the big guy was right beside me. I was scared, real scared. I'd seen my share of trouble in the eighteen months I'd been in 'Nam, but this was more trouble than I could handle and I knew it.

He looked at me, a hard piercing look that froze me in my tracks and searched my soul. I tried to talk, but I couldn't even move enough to breathe. Then he spoke, "When he grew up, he'd have to remember the senseless thing he'd done. It's better this way." His voice was like the rest of him, tan and dusty and hard. I nodded dumbly, and he turned and ran down the road in an easy loping stride.

I tried to watch him, but he seemed to dance in and out of sight like a mirage in the shadows. He just faded from view within a hundred yards, lost from sight in a jumble of huts.

Six months later I got out of 'Nam, leaving the war behind. At least I thought I was leaving it behind until I saw him in the crowd at Ft. Lewis...and panicked all over again.

I slid down the cinder block wall, keeping my back to its cool safety. I could feel the fear sweat running down my spine and soaking into my shirt. Then a hand gently shook my shoulder. I started a swing I knew would be useless, but stopped when I saw the concerned face of an older medic. "You all right, buddy? You looked real pale, there, like you'd seen a ghost or somethin'. You need help or anything? I got some quinine if you need it." He thought I was having an attack of malaria.

I shook my head and stumbled to my feet. My hands were shaking and my mouth felt dry. I don't remember just what it was I said, but I know it didn't make sense, not even to me.

That was nearly twenty years ago, twenty years that have been very good to me. I thought I'd put it all behind me. I mean, I'm not like those long-haired anachronisms you see on the street, still living in the sixties, still talking about 'Nam like it was yesterday instead of history.

History belongs in school books.

History does not belong in my office building.

You see, I rode up the elevator with him today. Just him and me for twenty-six floors. The elevator never stopped once the whole way.

I knew him immediately. It's those eyes, you see, the palest ice-blue I've ever seen. He's still got the tan, and it's real, not bought from a machine—you just know the difference.

He's still hard, too. He stood straight up, didn't lean on the wall or anything. When the elevator passed the twentieth floor, he slowly turned and looked at me, looked deep inside me. I felt like I was being measured for a coffin.

The most difficult thing I've ever done was to meet those terrible pale eyes. His expression never changed when he said in that tan and dusty voice, "We've all got something to live with. 'Nam was a long time ago and very far away."

For the second time in twenty years, I nodded dumbly to this man, my throat clogged with fear. I knew I'd be defenseless if he wanted me dead.

The elevator slid silently to a stop and the doors opened. With a tremendous effort, I broke the spell and asked as he stepped through, "Did you have to? I mean, was it necessary to..."

His pale eyes, those pale killer's eyes, slowly brimmed with tears. His jaw muscles writhed under his tan skin. "No," he said softly through clenched teeth, "none of it was."

The Goat

It felt like coming home.

The black naugahyde seats gleamed in welcome. The T-handle shifter squatted between the seats, the date I'd so carefully carved into it with the tip of my pocket knife worn but still visible.

I reached for the seat belt, knowing it would be twisted and buried under the seat, straightened it without looking, and snapped it tight. My fingers remembered how.

I slid the key into the slot, pumped the pedal twice, and turned her over. The '68 GTO, my old goat, started immediately, idling quietly and evenly, belying the muscle under the hood.

Years fell away, rolled back in layers like dusty film—each layer revealing a clearer view of how happy I'd been. Twenty years of living peeled away. Twenty years of picking up cares, some mine, some not.

I ran my fingers over the wheel, tracing the bumps on the back, stopped on the nearly smooth nick where I'd busted my tooth trying to get stopped before I hit a truck.

I grinned at the memory. Jenny'd slid down the seat, but her skirt hadn't. That was the first time I saw how beautiful her legs were. They still are, too, come to think of it.

My grin faded a little. I hadn't told her that in a long time.

I felt a little guilty about that, but she wasn't really putting out any effort either. That's why we had started talking about divorce. We both just seemed to be riding with things instead of trying.

God, they were good times in this car. We made love the first time in the back seat, so scared we'd be caught—all noses and elbows.

I crossed my hands on top of the wheel, conscious of the engine breathing and thrumming. She always seemed a part of me when I owned her, but that was eighteen long years ago. The car still looked good, sleek as a quarterhorse. She hadn't changed a bit.

Somehow, though, I had changed—and I missed me, the old me. I missed the guy who could laugh all night and take on the world on his own terms. I missed him a lot. I wish he hadn't died in Vietnam.

I took a deep breath. She even smelled the same, a faint blend of Lysol and Old Spice. The layers of years peeled back more and more. I started to see that maybe he wasn't entirely dead after all. The corners of my mouth lifted in a smile, a strange thing for me, at least a real smile was.

I turned her off, one of the hardest things I'd ever done, and handed the keys through the window to the kid who was trying to sell her.

"You want to take her for a spin?" He was no salesman, and he really didn't want to sell her. It showed clearly on his face.

I shook my head and managed to choke out, "No. No thanks."

"Am I charging too much? I mean, I owe almost a thousand on her, but if it's the price or something..."

I interrupted him. "It's not the price. Would you tell me why you want to sell her?"

"I don't, not really. She's a good car. It's just that I, I mean we, we're going to have a baby and I thought we should get something else. The payments are, well, you don't want to hear all this."

"I do, though. Is it a money problem?"

He nodded, not meeting my eyes in his shame.

"Can I tell you something?" I asked, and continued when he didn't stop me. "I was the first owner of this car. My dad helped me buy it in my senior year of high school. I loved her then, and I love her now, just like you do. Did you see the date carved into the shifter?"

He nodded, looking at me now. "I put it there the night I first made love to my wife. We aren't getting along too good right now, and a lot of that is my fault, but we've already been through our money problems.

"We'll do better on the other because I got to sit in my old goat. Maybe you'll understand that better someday if you're ever foolish enough to let the kid in you die out.

"What I'm trying to say is this. I do want to buy your car—at least for one night, and I'll make you a deal. If you'll loan me the car for tonight, I'll pay it off for you."

He opened his mouth to object, but I cut him off again. "Don't argue with me. I can afford it, and you'll be doing me more of a favor than you'll ever realize."

"You serious?" he asked. When I nodded, he said, "I don't know when I could pay you back, I mean..."

"You help somebody else down the line somewhere, that's all I ask."

He stuck out his hand and I took it. "Mister, you got yourself a deal."

Jenny came out the front door when I yelled, looking mildly perturbed. I scooped her up in my arms and ran across the lawn to where the goat shone by the curb. I set her down behind my old car—*our* old car—and handed her the keys.

"Are you out of your mind, Philip?" she asked, with years of protective chill in her voice.

"I brought you a present, Jenny."

"An old car?"

Then memories from the old days caught up with her. She looked down at the keys in her hand, then over at the trunk lid. The years faded away again as I watched the young girl I'd fallen in love with so long ago bend in slow motion, open the trunk, and lift out the dozen roses I'd picked up on the way home. Her chin peach-pitted and her eyes brimmed with tears. "Oh, Philly, they're beautiful."

I hadn't bought her roses in years, a mistake I never wanted to make again. She hadn't called me Philly for nearly as long. I didn't try to hide the tears I felt starting. "She still looks good after all these years, doesn't she?"

"My god, Philly, is it the same one?"

I nodded and watched the memories play in the back of her eyes. Strange, but I'd forgotten just how pretty her eyes were, such a deep brown.

"Would you like to go to a drive-in movie and start over? I think we can make it. I want us to make it."

She took a long time to answer, measuring me carefully, then she said, "I'd love a movie, Philly." Then she was in my arms, her tears wet on my cheek.

It felt like coming home.

Heroes

"Charlie, did I ever tell you about..."

My daddy, Charles Jameson, died when I was three years old. Mama told me I saw him three times, but I was too small to remember. So all I've ever had to remind me of him is my name (Charlene, or Charlie Junior, or sometimes even Junior for short), my freckles, and their wedding picture over the fireplace.

As I was growing up, Mama told me all about how her and Daddy fell in love: How they met at the Christmas dance when they were both sixteen; how they dumped their dates and spent the night talking in the back of his old Studebaker; how they got married before they were even out of high school, sneaking across the line into Kentucky so they didn't need permission, then springing the news on Mama's folks on graduation day. Gramps was so pissed off he wouldn't talk to Daddy 'til I was on the way, then he wouldn't shut up.

After Mama'd finish a story, I always wrote my own ending in my head: "And then he died." Only, last week I had to add another chapter to my ending: "And then she died, too."

Mama was only thirty-five, but the cancer didn't care. She wouldn't tell me about it until she couldn't stand up straight from the way it was eating her up inside; I got her to the doctor, but he said she'd waited too long and he couldn't do anything. He gave me something to ease her pain and told me to take her home.

Somehow, knowing she was going to die seemed to open Mama up even more. Always before, she wouldn't ever tell me much about how Daddy died, only that they loved each other somethin' fierce and that she missed him every day. I knew he was on his third tour when it happened, and that he'd promised it'd be his last, but she wouldn't say anything more. She'd packed me up and moved me back to their hometown, to the house Gram and Gramps had left her.

But now, she started telling me day-by-day what their life was like, like I was a journal she was filling. I took some time off from the stable where I work to take care of her, and sat beside her for hours at a time. "Junior," she'd say, "did I ever tell you how you came into this world?" And I'd say, "No, Mama, you tell me." I'd heard most of the stories before, but I just wanted to keep on hearing her voice. I already knew we didn't have long, and she must have known it, too.

One day toward the end, Mama came out of her drowse and fumbled for my hand. When she found it, she fisted hers around it with a grip like ice.

"Charlene," she whispered, and my heart froze. She never called me Charlene, and I was scared.

"Charlene, listen to me. There's something I got to tell you about your daddy." I tried to quiet her down, but her iron grip didn't loosen.

"Don't you shush me, just listen. I've done a terrible thing and I want it off my soul before I go.

"Your daddy...your daddy was a hero, and don't you ever let anybody tell you different. But he died a tired-out and scared man, and I couldn't ever tell you before."

She stopped a moment, gasping for the breath that never came easy now, but glared me silent through her tears when I tried to speak.

"Your daddy went to that godawful war a wonderful man, but he came home changed." She felt my hand jump in hers and tightened her grip. All at once I knew I didn't want to hear this, but she wouldn't let me go.

"Yes, I said 'came home.' He served his three tours all right, then he came home to me, full of death and pain. He went to the VA docs a couple times, but they wouldn't do anything to help. His soul'd been torn to bits and they couldn't see it on an x-ray or reach it with a knife, so they just gave him drugs to forget with and sent him away.

"Except the drugs only worked for a while, then the nightmares'd come back. Twice he woke up with his fist through the wall by our bed, and my poor darling was so scared 'cause he loved you and me so much and knew he'd end up hurting us. He never would've wanted to, but the war was going to make him and he couldn't find any way to stop it.

"So one day, when I was gone with you to the doctor, he found a way. He stopped himself, for good and all. And he did it out of love."

I just sat there, my left hand clenched in her right, and felt the blood drain right out of me. He killed himself? How could she lie to me all these years? I tried to wrench myself away from this skeleton on the bed, telling me painful truths when I was already overflowing with pain. I'm already hurting, I wanted to scream at her. You're dying, why do you have to hurt me more than that?

From some inner reserve, Mama found the strength to pull me down into her arms. I'm a strong girl, used to slinging bales of hay and controlling racehorses, but this tiny, bone-thin, dying woman held me. Somehow, I never doubted the truth of her words; they echoed inside me like church bells, and my pain knew they were true.

When my tears finally ran out, Mama released me just far enough to see my face.

"You listen to me, Junior. Your daddy was a hero, no matter what you think of him—or me—now. That war killed him, as sure as if a bullet had split his brain, but it didn't kill him clean. It sent him home to die slow, and maybe to take someone he loved with him. All he did was try to clean up what was left, and he did just fine, you hear me! I'm the one what screwed it up, 'cause I couldn't figure out how to tell you, but now that's set to rights.

"Your daddy did an honorable thing, and I hope you're lucky enough to find a man with half the heart he had."

Mama lay back on the bed again, tears running down her pale, thin cheeks. She reached up her free hand and brushed my hair back behind my ears. I sat there with her, holding her hand and stroking her cheek, until she drifted off to sleep again.

I went home after she died, and just sat in front of the fireplace all night, staring at their wedding picture on the mantle.

Hello, Grant

"Hello, my name is Grant, and I'm an alcoholic."

"Hello, Grant," in unison.

"Special congratulations are in order for some of our members tonight. As most of you regulars know, we give out ribbons to mark progress—a different color for each year we've been sober."

He paused a moment to take a sip from his cup, coffee black and sweet, then took a drag off his cigarette. Thirty or so people watched him silently through the haze of smoke, hanging on his every word. He took a shaky breath as he reached into the cardboard box in front of him, then continued.

"We want to help Frank over here," he gestured with the hand holding the blue ribbon, "celebrate one full year without a drink. Frank, will you come up here and get your ribbon and tell us all about it?"

Frank slid his chair back slowly and walked around the end of the table. He took the ribbon from Grant's hand and held it up in the dim light, a proud grin spreading over his face. "I never thought..."

A voice called from the back of the room, "Who are you?"

Frank grinned even wider, embarrassed. "Hello, my name is Frank, and I'm an alcoholic."

"Hello, Frank," in unison.

"Like I was just sayin', I never thought I would make it to this day. I gotta tell you, I could sure use a drink to celebrate. But this is just one more day to make it through. Just today, that's all. If I can just stay dry today, I'm going to do all right."

The group broke into a ragged applause, and Frank held up his hand for quiet. "It's for you guys, you know. I wouldn't have made it this far without you. Thanks—thanks for saving my life."

He turned to return to his seat, and the applause followed him all the way back. Pride and embarrassment mixed on his face as he sat back down, showing his ribbon to the man sitting next to him.

Grant spoke as the applause died down: "Peggy over here, well, she's been dry for five years, this week. Peggy, come on up here and tell us about it."

Peggy rose and rushed forward eagerly. She rose on tiptoe to kiss Grant on the cheek when he handed her the ribbon, then turned to face the rest of the group. She dug a Kleenex from her pocket and dabbed at her eyes as she said, "Hello, I'm Peggy, and I'm an alcoholic."

"Hello, Peggy," in unison.

"I want to thank all of you for helping me make it this far." She laughed nervously, "I—I—well, I never thought I'd ever make it this far." They laughed with her. "It's been a very long five years, long and hard. But I want you to know that if I can make it, so can you. Make it through today, just today, and someday soon, you'll get a red ribbon like this, too. All it takes is one day at a time."

Peggy rose up on her toes to kiss Grant again, then practically ran back to her chair while the group applauded for her.

Grant looked down at the table, down into the box in front of him, for a long quiet moment. His eyes were shiny with tears when he looked up. "Does anybody have something they'd like to share?"

They knew then, and you could almost hear their collective heartbeat falter. They knew, and they waited for him in silent dread. He was their hero, their leader—he'd sponsored many of them, cried with them, held them when the shakes and the need grew so strong they couldn't hold out by themselves. He was their friend.

Grant cleared his throat, the sound abrasive in the silence. "I've been sober for two days." The tears welled in his eyes, then trickled slowly down his cheeks. They waited for him—hurt for him.

"Six days ago, they told me..." he fought past the thickness in his throat "...they told me that David, my oldest son, was shot down over Iraq. Missing in action, they said. Missing..."

Peggy jumped to her feet and rushed forward. Grant waved her off and she backed away, tears streaking her face.

"My first thoughts were that it couldn't really be true. They had to be lying to me somehow—for some reason. I got mad, I guess. I don't remember it too well. Jenny, my wife, tried to calm me down, tried hard, but she just seemed to make it worse. And I walked out on her. I walked out and got drunk.

"You see, all I could think of was David dead. Another stupid war, and David dead because I let it happen. Because I didn't—because I—it's my fault, you see. I should've done something.

"I should've—but I didn't. I hid from what happened to me in Vietnam, acted like it never..."

Grant shook out a cigarette and held a light to it with shaky hands. "Maybe if I hadn't crawled into a bottle when I got back, maybe David'd still be alive. Maybe he would've listened and not gone over there.

"But we didn't get along very well. He calls his mother every now and then—or he did before this happened. But he wouldn't even talk to me.

"And when they told me he was shot down, I guess I just lost it. It felt like it was all a waste, you see."

Grant held up the yellow ribbon he would have received for ten years dry. "And now he's gone. Maybe dead. I let him down all his life, and now I've got to let him down again. Just a few days, a few more days, and I could've flown a yellow ribbon for his safe return. Just a few more days..."

Grant took a deep shaky breath, lifted his head to face the group, and said: "My name is Grant, and I'm an alcoholic. I've been dry for two days."

Flame Out

"Will you marry me?"

Ray's nerves were stretched as tight as bailing wire. He'd spent weeks working up the nerve to ask, and Marcia's frown wasn't encouraging.

"No. I'm sorry," she said.

"Well, why the hell not?" Ray's patience blew like an old tire. "Don't you love me? I mean, Christ, we've been living together for three years. Doesn't that mean anything to you?" He knew he was yelling, but he couldn't help himself. Some part of him recognized the finality in her answer, and he couldn't bear it.

"Yes, I do love you. I've told you that before." Marcia spoke slowly and calmly, the same reasoning tone she used with the show horses she trained. "I can't marry you because I am married. I can love you, I can make love with you, I can even live with you, but I won't marry you."

"Steve's dead, Mar; you're a widow, not a wife."

"Ray, 'missing in action' means just that: missing. Steve's alive, and he will some day come home." Marcia's warm brown eyes gazed steadily into Ray's overflowing blues, and her words drove a nail through his heart.

"You mean to tell me, if Steve walked up the driveway tomorrow, you'd go with him, just like that?"

"Yes."

"I don't understand you. I thought we were building something here, something important, maybe even something forever."

"You're a nice man and you've been very kind to me. We've kept each other warm on some really cold nights, and been through some rough times together. I'll always care about you. Isn't that enough?"

"'Kind!' Is that all you thought it was? Jesus, I know you've always held back, but I figured it was just a matter of time. I want to marry you, have kids together, spend the rest of our lives together. Why can't you see that?"

Marcia stood up and walked to the window, staring for a moment at the old oak tree that shaded the walk. Without turning back, she spoke to the man who sat sobbing at the kitchen table, his head in his hands.

"This isn't easy to say, because I've never thought out the words before. Loves come in different shapes and sizes. You're a very sweet man and I really do love you. But Steve and I have something so much more that 'love' doesn't even describe it. We're...soulmates, I guess you'd say."

Her certainty was more than Ray's shattered emotions could stand. He burst from his cane chair, grabbing her shoulders and turning her to face him.

"Steve's dead! He's been dead for fifteen fucking years! His goddamn plane flamed out and crashed! No matter how many pension checks you tear up, no matter how many letters you write to Hanoi, Steve is DEAD! The Army knows it, I know it, and you should goddamn well know it by now. What's it gonna take to convince you?!"

She just looked at him, not even wincing from his fingers dug into her arms. They stared at each other until Ray finally let go and dropped his hands to his sides.

As he turned away, Marcia said: "If Steve were dead, I'd know it. Until I do, I'm married." Ray didn't show he'd heard, just wandered from the kitchen. Marcia washed the dishes, then went into the bedroom to pack.

Jimi

He caught the phone on its first ring, irritably snatching it from the cradle. "Doctor Hendrix," he snapped into the receiver. He had cause to be irritable. It was nearly midnight, and his departmental budget report was due tomorrow. Everybody likely to call knew this. He'd even sent his family over to Eve's mother's for the evening so he could get his work done.

"Jimi?" The voice on the other end sounded tentative, scared.

It was the music in the background at the other end that made the connection in his mind, Janis Joplin pouring her soul and about a triple shot of Southern Comfort into *Cry Baby*. Nobody like her, before or since.

And nobody called him "Jimi" any more. "Walter," if they knew him well, or "Doctor Hendrix," but never "Jimi." That was Scott's joke. He started it and the others in the platoon just seemed to follow along, calling their medic "Jimi" because of his last name.

"Jimi? That you, bro?"

"Scott?" Just uttering the name tore twenty years of protective layers from his soul.

"Yeah, bro. One and the same."

"Where are you? You in town?"

"Yeah, bro, I'm in a town."

Hendrix pushed the stack of papers away from him, and swung his feet up onto his desk. "You are one crazy motherfucker, Scott. What the hell town are you in?"

"Detroit." Over a thousand miles from where Hendrix sat in Atlanta.

"Well, you coming this way? It'd be great to see you again."

"I think I'll be staying right where I am, Jimi. This is as good a spot as any."

Something in the way Scott said it, the undercurrent of despair, set Walter's teeth on edge. "You all right, Scott? You sound sort of, well, strange."

Scott was silent for a moment. "I didn't call you to lay my troubles on you, bro. I was just sitting here in my room, thinking about that time in 'Nam when you hauled me out of that VC camp."

They were both prisoners, then, and the VC had worked them over pretty good. Scott was all shot up, and Hendrix hadn't expected him to live for long. But when he saw his chance, he grabbed Scott and made a run for it.

"Nothin' to it, Scott. You'd of done the same for me."

"Never got to pay you back for that one, Jimi. You coulda made it easy without me, but no—you gotta carry me over half the goddamn country with gooks crawlin' the bushes around us. Heavy shit, bro."

"Hey, it don't mean a thing."

"I just want you to know you're my friend, and I'm your friend. You done good."

"It's past, Scott. Let's just leave it there."

"You see, bro, that's where the trouble is. I can't leave it there. I still wake up at night runnin' sweat and scared. I catch myself holding my breath so Charlie won't hear me. I can't leave it there. It's right here with me."

Dr. Hendrix thought quickly. "Have you tried one of those vet centers? I've read some very good reports on them."

"I been to the vet centers, bro. I been to the VA. I been to the shrinks. I been to every damn place there is. They all tell me I can forget it. But I can't. I got the whole damn war riding around on my back like a monkey. I can't shake it loose. I can't forget it. I can't drink it away. I can't...ah, hell, Jimi. You sound so much like a doctor you got me sounding like a damn patient. I just wanted to tell you thanks for saving my life. I mean it, man."

"Ain't no big thing, bro," Jimi said.

"I just didn't want you to hear about it from somebody else and think you done something wrong, man. You done a good thing, and don't you forget it."

"Hear about what, bro?"

"I can't think of any other way to get that damn war out of my head, Jimi. Stay with me 'til it's over...please."

"Scotty! Don't be talking shit! If you're saying what I think you mean..."

"Yeah, bro. I just can't take it no more."

"You can't do this. I'll fly up there tonight, buddy. You and me, we can talk it out. We can do it, just like in the 'Nam."

"You can't carry me home from this one, bro. There just ain't no home no more."

Jimi recognized the finality in Scott's voice and leaned back in his chair. "So what do you want from me?"

"Remember how you talked to me? You just wouldn't shut up. You talked your ever-lovin' ass off, all the while dragging me through the goddamn jungle. I was hurtin' man, but you made me real. You kept the pieces together."

"What are you getting at, Scotty?"

"I need you to keep the pieces together, bro. One last time. You and me, we been to the shit. Just keep the pieces together."

"I don't know what you mean."

"There ain't nobody else, man. No old lady. No people. Somebody's got to remember me. Somebody's got to hold onto the pieces."

"I'll remember, bro. You held me together then, too. I would've given up if it wasn't for you. I owe you, too."

"Thanks, man."

"You really in Detroit?"

"Yeah."

"Gimme an address."

Scott was immediately suspicious. "So you can call the cops?"

"No. So I can come and carry your ugly ass home."

"You'd do that for me?"

"For us, bro. We're in this together."

Scott gave him the address. "Well, bro, I guess this is it. I love you, bro."

"I love you, too. And I won't forget. I promise."

"Stay with me?"

"No sweat."

The phone line was quiet for several long moments, then Scotty spoke again, very softly. "Bye, bro."

Even expecting it, the boom of the shot surprised Jimi. He jumped at the noise, then as he settled back down, heard the sound of Scotty's body hitting the floor. He listened intently for any other sound, but all he heard was the record come to an end. Scotty was dead.

Eve stopped in front of the house for a moment, feeling the pounding music shake the fillings in her teeth. Steppenwolf. No doubt about it. *Born To Be Wild.*

She thought it over quickly and drove back to her mother's house. Promising to explain later, she dropped the kids off to spend the night, and was back home in less than twenty minutes. This time, she turned the motor off and went in.

She found Walter where she thought she'd find him, sitting on the roof in the dark, the huge stereo speakers booming out the window. She climbed out onto the roof and settled down beside him. He didn't appear to notice her for a very long time.

When the record ended, she said, "'Been a good fifteen years since you came out here like this. Do you want to talk?"

He shook his head, but then after a long pause, said, "I'm flying to Detroit in the morning."

She waited for him to continue.

"I've got to go pick up a friend."

"Can't your friend just fly down here?"

"Not any more. Not by himself. He's dead."

"Dead!? Who is it?"

"A guy I knew in 'Nam. The war finally killed him tonight."

"I don't understand."

"Hard to, unless you was in the shit. We were, him and me. Deep shit. The only difference is, I got out."

"What's his name?"

He forced the words out. "Let me tell you about Scotty."

Vigil

He was the first to arrive, a tall gaunt man, long-haired, and silent. He sat on the dew-damp grass, back from the crowd of visitors and gazed thoughtfully at the bleak ebon scar carved into the gentle rise of land.

Throughout the day, only his eyes moved as he watched the crowd stream past the Wall. His face an expressionless mask, he seemed to absorb the tears and emotional turmoil around him.

Saturday dawned and found two other men seated with him. One wore the four-starred patch of the Americal Division on a faded fatigue jacket. Others drifted in through the day until a ragtag bunch of thirteen sat silently in the dawn of Easter Sunday.

As dusk settled over the hill, they rose and kicked the kinks out of their legs and left without a word. Nobody noticed them, thirteen silent men aloof from the crowd.

But they were back on the next Good Friday to renew their vigil. And people noticed. They had to, for each of the thirteen brought a hundred silent watchers to spread out on the hillside. A lone man, moustache to the bottom of his chin, came to ask what the party was, but sat down without a word.

By ones and twos they came. Men, women, veterans, non-veterans. Easter dawn found eleven thousand people sitting silently, monitored by thirty nervous police.

When the sun sank behind the horizon, thirteen thousand people stood, brushed themselves off, and drifted silently away.

Sunset on the third Easter found nearly sixty thousand people there and the first man stood as the sun touched the horizon. Three years, and not one of them had spoken. Sixty thousand faces turned to hear what he had to say.

He appeared to grope for the words, but his voice carried softly above the crowd. "There's about one of us here for each of them," he said.

And then he began to sing, and his rich baritone rolled out over the crowd, and over the silent names carved into the black granite.

Amazing Grace, how sweet the sound.

And sixty thousand voices joined in.